UNDER
THE
ICE BLADES

BOOK 5.5

LINDSAY BUROKER

Under the Ice Blades

by Lindsay Buroker

Copyright @ Lindsay Buroker 2015

Cover and Formatting: Deranged Doctor Design

ACKNOWLEDGMENTS

After I finished the fifth Dragon Blood novel, I planned to take a break from the series, but the characters wouldn't stop popping into my head, sharing snippets of dialogue and telling me about their escapades. I soon came up with ideas for Book Six and for this story, an adventure starring Captain Kaika and a certain male character that we hadn't heard much from yet. I had intended Under the Ice Blades to be a side story, one not crucial to read for those following along with the series, but a new "problem" arose in this one, and we'll see it again in Book Six, so I'm glad you're checking out this adventure! We'll also have more of Cas and Tolemek in Book Six—I know some of you are wondering what's going to happen with Cas after the events in Book Five. That will be answered soon, but in the meantime, I hope you'll enjoy this story.

As always, before you jump in, I would like to thank my beta readers, Cindy Wilkinson and Sarah Engelke, my editor, Shelley Holloway, and the cover designer for this series, Deranged Doctor Design. And thank you, good readers, for following along!

CHAPTER 1

C APTAIN KAIKA KEPT HERSELF FROM running down the corridor of the Nightclaw Infantry Brigade's headquarters, but only because numerous colonels and generals were wandering about, holding stacks of papers and carrying coffee mugs, their eyes still bleary with sleep. She tossed quick salutes as she weaved past them, feeling none of their enervation, even though she had been up most of the night celebrating life—and the impressive strength and flexibility of one of General Zirkander's handsome flier mechanics.

Who could be tired when a new mission was on the horizon?

She came to a halt in front of General Braksonoth's door, quivering with the anticipation of a hunting dog on point. Where would she be sent this time? Would she be assigned a new partner? The elite forces teams almost always worked in pairs, especially overseas. Who might she be assigned? More importantly, where would she be going? It had been nearly three weeks since she had helped Zirkander, Sardelle, and the others free the king and drive off the Cofah invasion. That was an eternity of time to loiter in the rear without a purpose.

Her knock had the enthusiasm and force of a small explosion.

"Come in, Captain," the general's voice came through the door, soft and dry.

Kaika tried to march in with stately decorum, but she couldn't keep from bouncing on her toes as she came to attention on the rug in front of the desk. Getting a new mission was better than fifteen-year-aged takva, better than sex, and even better than blowing up enemy strongholds. Of course, a new mission often *led* to blowing up enemy strongholds, so that was part of the appeal. But the constant element of danger kept her more alert and alive than she ever was back at home.

"Reporting for duty, sir." Kaika gave the general a much more professional salute than the ones she had tossed in the corridor. Unlike the rest of the officers in the building, Braksonoth, commander of the intelligence battalion, held her fate in his hands. Even though the elite forces teams were technically a part of the infantry brigade and often worked in conjunction with the combat soldiers, they received orders from this man. "Do you have a new mission, sir?" she couldn't help but add.

Braksonoth folded his hands on his desk and gazed blandly up at her through his spectacles. The soft-spoken, gray-haired officer weighed less than a hundred and fifty pounds and looked up at six-foot-tall Kaika even when they were both standing, but she knew better than to underestimate him. She'd seen his record, the part that wasn't classified. He had been on over a hundred spy missions, taken down critical enemy fortifications, and survived countless battles that others on his teams hadn't walked away from. He knew everything about this job, and he could send her on the most amazing missions... or he could send her to the kitchens to mash turnips. She'd done both for him in her fifteen years in the unit.

"I have new orders for you." Braksonoth licked his finger and slid the top sheet of paper off a stack.

"Orders, sir?"

Orders weren't a mission. Orders were a... who knew what? A transfer to a new army fort or to a training school. But she'd been to all of the training schools. And why would her superiors send her to another fort? The elite forces had always been based out of the capital.

"Orders." Braksonoth turned the paper and laid it on the desk so she could read the typed page. "You're to report to General Zirkander. The air division is expanding, and he's selected a number of new pilots to graduate early from the academy. You'll be training them in combat and incursion and survival tactics."

Kaika stared at the page, though those little black type marks were blurring before her eyes. "*Training*, sir? You want me to train a bunch of mouthy kids? Mouthy kid pilots at that? What do they know about incursion and combat? They just sit up there in their flying boxes."

Complaining about orders wasn't seemly, especially to one's C.O., but what was he *thinking*? Teaching was for old or injured veterans that were close to retirement. You didn't send a field officer in the prime of her life into a classroom. What a waste! She squinted at the orders, as if she might find another name typed across the top, as if this might all be a mistake. But no, her entire name, including the first name she loathed, was there: Captain Astuawilda Kaika.

"Apparently, those flying boxes get shot down on occasion," Braksonoth said, "and they need to know what to do when that happens."

"But, *sir*. Why *me*? I'm not any good at teaching. I don't have the patience for it."

"Perhaps this will allow you to cultivate a new skill." His tone had grown a shade cooler. He might not be as hard assed as someone like Colonel Therrik, but he wouldn't let her argue with him, either. "If not for a few impulsive decisions in your career, you might have achieved a higher rank than captain by now."

But she didn't *want* a higher rank. Or at least she didn't care one way or another about it. She just wanted to go on missions.

Even though arguing wasn't wise, she couldn't bring herself to accept the assignment without a fight. "Is it possible there's been a mistake, sir? Did—did General Zirkander *request* me?"

That thought brought a sliver of hope. Even though she couldn't imagine why he would have done so, if the orders had originated with Zirkander, he might be convinced to reverse them. They had worked together, and he was a reasonable man. She could talk to him, make a request. Zirkander hadn't wanted to accept his promotion because he had worried it would take him out of the sky and pin him to a desk. Surely, he could understand if she was afflicted by a similar dread. Seven gods, this teaching job might even come with paperwork. That would almost be worse than dealing with mouthy kids straight out of the academy. She might be able to defuse a daisy chain of bombs in less than five minutes, but she couldn't type without getting her fingers tangled up in the keys.

"No," Braksonoth said. "Your orders came directly from King Angulus."

Kaika nearly fell over. "The *king*? Why would he have anything to do with... That's not normal, is it?"

"No, it's not. He generally trusts us to handle our own personnel assignments."

"Is it because I winked at him at that dinner celebration at the castle? This isn't a punishment, is it?" Kaika had doubted the king had even noticed that wink, but as soon as the word *punishment* came out of her mouth, a wrecking ball of realization crashed into her.

Not the wink. That was nothing. She winked at every man who was worthy. But how could she have forgotten the role she had played during that fiasco of an infiltration with Sardelle and Lieutenant Ahn? The explosion in the castle. The queen's *death*. Even if the king and queen hadn't been reputed to be close, and even if the queen had been the mastermind responsible for his kidnapping, that didn't mean that he hadn't had feelings for her after twenty years of marriage. Angulus might have been polite at the dinner celebration, but he was *always* polite, in his dry, eyes-piercing-your-soul kind of way. Who knew what had actually been going on in his mind? What if he resented her for blowing up his castle? And his *wife*. Just because she had been trying to find and rescue him at the time didn't make anything about that nightmare of a night acceptable.

"I wasn't told why he chose to assign you there," Braksonoth said, "merely given the orders. You report to General Zirkander at 0900 hours this morning. I suggest you don't wink at *him*. We've spent a lot on your training. It would be unfortunate if his witch vaporized you."

Kaika snorted. Sardelle was a healer; she wouldn't vaporize anyone, even if she could. Kaika was more worried about the king and what he thought of her. He had the power to ensure she never went on another mission again. How in all the hells was she supposed to make sure that didn't happen?

* * *

"Go, go, go, you vulture kissers," Kaika shouted to the cadets laboring to pull themselves up the fifteen-foot wooden wall on the obstacle course. "How did you graduate from the flight program without knowing how to climb anything higher than a warthog? Don't you have to be able to get up and *in* to your fliers?"

Nothing but grunts and groans answered her, and those were muffled by the spring rain spattering into mud puddles all over the course.

"Maxton, you better go back and help your partner over that wall," Kaika yelled. "You're not going to stand a chance against the Cofah guardian waiting at the end if you don't have help." She prodded her chest with a thumb, to remind them that she was playing the role of guardian for this exercise. After standing around going hoarse and being rained on for the last hour, she welcomed the chance for some action, even if it was pretend action on a pretend battlefield.

The cadet she had yelled at—Maxton, or was it Madton?—glared bullets at her. He probably wouldn't mind a chance to come at her with his fists swinging. He would have to wait his turn. Two other cadets were low crawling through the mud, logs, and netting that marked the end of the course. Kaika backed up, giving them room to get up before they tried to get past her. They would have to knock her down or shove her out of the way to pass through the wood tunnel that separated them from their final destination, a stump with a toy dragon on it—it symbolized one of their fliers. If they touched it within the three minutes they had to finish the course, they could pretend they had evaded capture and could escape. So far, nobody had even managed to reach her before the three minutes ran out. These two looked like they would make it.

The male cadet outpaced his female partner under the netting and clambered to his feet first. Instead of waiting for her, or reaching back to help her, he charged straight at Kaika.

Maybe he thought he could catch her by surprise. Whatever his plan was, it didn't work. Compared to some of the soldiers she'd fought, he seemed to be moving at half speed, with his exaggerated movements easier to read than messages coming in on a telegraph machine.

She dodged to the side to avoid his lunging punch and batted aside his arm with a forearm block at the same time as she stepped in and slammed an upper cut into the soft flesh under his ribcage. She finished with a knee to the groin before he could recover. He crumpled forward, and she dropped her elbow onto his upper back to help him to the ground. He roared with pain and frustration as he splatted into the mud at her feet.

Kaika kept an eye on him as she regarded his female partner. The slender figure reminded her of Lieutenant Ahn, at least in her diminutive size, but her eyes were round with wariness and apprehension, not cool and calm with calculation. She came forward, more because the exercise demanded it and time was ticking down than because she wanted to; at least, that was what her expression said. Kaika blocked a few tentative punches, letting the cadet gain some experience before turning defense to offense. In the end, the young woman lay in the mud next to her partner.

"Had you attacked together," Kaika said, "you might have had a chance. At the least, one could have distracted me or drawn me away from the tunnel, so the other could have gotten away to report back. Someone *always* has to make it out to report back."

A memory flashed through her mind of a time not that long ago when someone had said the same thing to her. Back in the Cofah volcano base, Captain Nowon, her partner of more than five years, had ordered her to leave him behind after he'd been mortally wounded by a trap. He'd gone down fighting, so she had the time to slip away, to finish their mission and rejoin the others. To this day, she wondered why she'd been the one to make it when he hadn't. He'd always been the smart one, the patient one, the better soldier. Maybe the king wasn't the only one punishing Kaika with this new assignment. Maybe fate had decided she needed to learn a lesson. Patience? Was that it? Her mother had tried to teach her that as a child, but it had never stuck.

"We're pilots, ma'am," the male cadet said, glowering at her from the mud, not bothering to climb to his feet to address her. An infantry cadet wouldn't have been so blasé when speaking to a superior officer. "When are we ever going to have to face a Cofah berserker?"

"Pilots get shot down and get captured," said a male voice from behind Kaika. "It's happened to me, and it's happened very recently to Lieutenant Ahn."

The cadet's eyes widened, and he scrambled to his feet so quickly, he almost fell over again.

"Sir," he blurted, looking mortified, as if he'd just been caught napping instead of getting knocked on his ass. He locked himself into a rigid attention stance, as the female cadet and everyone else on the course did the same. "I know, sir. I mean, I didn't know, sir. I mean—uhm. Sorry, sir."

Kaika turned and offered a salute of her own, though she doubted Zirkander would notice or care if she didn't. He strolled up, mud spattering his boots, the fur collar of his leather flight jacket turned up against the rain. It hid his rank pins, but nobody in this group would fail to recognize him. For that matter, he was such a darling of the newspapers, there weren't many people in the country who wouldn't recognize him.

Zirkander returned the cadet's salute, then made a shooing motion. "Go clean something, cadet. Yourself perhaps."

A chagrined expression flashed across the young man's face as he glanced down at his mud-drenched uniform, but he answered with a prompt, "Yes, sir," and darted away. The female cadet hurried away, too, moving quietly, as if she didn't want to be noticed. Her performance hadn't been *that* poor; the young man had more to be chagrined about.

"Take two minutes," Kaika called out to the rest of them.

"You're only going to allot me two minutes of your time?" Zirkander asked with a smirk.

"Maybe three," she said, smirking back before she caught herself.

The number of enemy aircraft he had shot down wasn't the

only reason the papers loved him. Zirkander was one of the most handsome men in the army, and Kaika knew without a doubt that thousands of photos from his numerous newspaper articles had been clipped out and stuck to the iceboxes of housewives all over Iskandia. The barest hint of a smile could set a girl's libido to humming, and it was very hard *not* to return his smirks. Even if he hadn't been devotedly canoodling with Sardelle, Kaika knew she wouldn't have had a shot with him. She might have tried anyway if he and Sardelle hadn't been so obviously smitten with each other. Instead, she kept her demeanor professional— mostly—and managed not to wink at him.

"How is Lieutenant Ahn doing?" Kaika asked quietly.

All trace of his humor evaporated. "She finally managed to find someone to accept her resignation papers."

"Oh." Kaika didn't know what else to say. It hadn't been being shot down and captured that had squashed Ahn's spirits; no, she had been a part of that same castle infiltration that had left the queen dead. Under the influence of a semi-sentient magical sword, she'd killed one of her colleagues, and she couldn't forgive herself for that. Kaika could understand, because she felt guilty over Nowon's death, even if she hadn't been responsible. She knew what it was like to survive when an equally capable—or *more* capable—comrade did not.

"Yeah." Zirkander sighed. "But I haven't given up hope. Earlier this week, I sent her the schematics for the new models of dragon fliers we've got in production. I even dragged a photographer out to the hangar to take pictures of the machine guns to include."

"You really know how to charm a woman, sir."

"Funny, my mother said the same thing. Only with even more sarcasm."

"It's probably a good thing that you're pretty."

He gave her a sidelong look. "I prefer ruggedly handsome."

"I'm sure you do." A wink slipped out. Damn it. She was *not* flirting with her happily paired C.O.

He didn't seem to notice. She told herself that was good, not depressing.

Zirkander tilted his chin toward the course. "Any of the youngsters looking promising?"

"Compared to what?" Kaika asked before a more diplomatic answer could form on her tongue. Diplomacy wasn't her forte.

"Well. You've seen Colonel Therrik manhandle me. Our ground combat standards aren't that high."

Kaika snorted. "Therrik manhandles everybody."

One of his eyebrows twitched, and she caught her cheeks flushing slightly. She'd had a brief—extremely brief—dalliance with the grumpy colonel a few years earlier. He had extremely lickable abs and an ass that—well, that didn't matter. Those body parts were attached to a man with the personality of a cannonball, and her only defense was that she had been horny, and alcohol had been involved.

Reminding herself that Zirkander hadn't actually said anything—maybe his eyebrow was just itchy—she decided to move the conversation on from manhandling. "Have you gone to visit him yet? Now that you're *General* Zirkander?"

"Therrik? No, he's up commanding the two-mile-high Magroth Crystal Mines post." Zirkander flashed an edged grin. "I *have* considered going out for an inspection, just so he'd have to show me around and yes-sir me."

"Do the mines fall under your domain now?"

"Nah. This is my domain." He waved toward the pilots who were toweling off under a tree, though he cast a longing look toward the cloudy sky over the harbor where a squadron of fliers buzzed about performing aerial maneuvers. "And yours, too, I suppose. Odd as that is." He gave her a quizzical look. He didn't think she had requested this assignment, did he?

"Yes, about that, sir. I was wondering if you knew—uhm, I was told the king was responsible for my orders. Do you know anything about it? I'd rather not be the one to pummel your flying puppies into the ground on a daily basis."

"Are you this candid with all of your senior officers?"

"Aren't you?"

"Well, yes, but I'm told my military manner shouldn't be used as a model."

He reputedly got away with a lot because he was the best pilot in the sky. Yet, he'd still made general at forty. Kaika was one of the best soldiers at what *she* did, but that never seemed to translate into promotions. It was a good thing she didn't *want* more responsibility or to end up in charge of teams instead of *on* teams.

"Do you think you could talk to him, sir?" Maybe if she pummeled enough of his cadets into the ground, they would complain, and Zirkander would see the merits of requesting someone more serene for the teaching position.

"The king? We're not really best buddies."

"I thought you were best buddies with everyone, sir."

"Only those who appreciate my irrepressible charm."

Oh? From what Kaika had noticed, King Angulus had a dry manner that might turn to laughs if one could ever catch him relaxed and off duty. But did kings ever get to *be* off duty? She wasn't sure she could imagine him sitting at a bar and swilling beers with Zirkander, but he seemed like he'd be more likely to appreciate Zirkander's bluntness, however irrepressible, than the attitudes of men who chose diplomacy—and prevarication— with him. Still, what did she know? When Kaika had been recounting—*confessing*—the events of the queen's death after Zirkander had recovered him from the kidnappers, she hadn't received the impression that Angulus blamed her, hated her, or otherwise wanted to punish her. Yet here she was.

Zirkander's gaze shifted past her shoulder, toward an elevated walkway and bleachers that overlooked the muddy training field. "You may get a chance to talk to the king yourself."

Kaika followed his gaze and spotted King Angulus and four bodyguards standing on the walkway. He leaned against the railing, looking out over the obstacle course and the harbor beyond it. Perhaps due to the drizzle, he wore none of the trappings of office, being dressed only in practical boots, trousers, and an oilskin jacket and cap to repel water. Even without kingly accoutrements, there was no mistaking his tall and broad build or his face, which included a square jaw, deep brown eyes that noticed everything, and short, curly hair that was more gray than brown these days. He was in his mid-forties, and any woman would find him handsome, though perhaps not in the take-a-second-look-to-adequately-fuel-later-fantasies way that Zirkander was. Had he been a mechanic or soldier she'd met in a bar, she might have had a chance at luring him off for an evening of carnal pleasures, but whoever kings had carnal pleasures with, it wasn't mud-spattered field officers.

After giving them a nod, Angulus headed for stairs that led down to the field.

"I'm sure he's here to talk to *you*, sir," Kaika said.

"Probably here to see if any of the cadets look promising. Most of them should still be in the academy, but with the elevated Cofah threat, we need to get more qualified pilots in the air." Zirkander waved at her before heading toward the bottom of the stairs. "You better get them back to work. And try to make them look good for the king, will you?"

"Good? It's my first day here, sir. Eventually, I might be able to convert them from so-embarrassing-they-trip-over-their-own-boots to awkward-but-with-potential. That day isn't here yet, and *good* is an extremely distant goal."

"Do your best."

While Zirkander spoke with the king, Kaika rounded up the troops and started more teams through the obstacle course. She kept an eye on Angulus, planning to run up and ask for an audience before he left. It was presumptuous, but it wouldn't be the first time she had been presumptuous with him. Early in her military career, she had earned her spot in the elite forces program, a program that had never been open to women, after blowing up an urn in the castle to demonstrate to the king that she would make a fine addition to the demolitions unit. She had never known if Angulus, fresh to the throne after his father's death back then, had found her antics bold and admirable or appalling and inappropriate. Either way, he'd seen fit to give her special permission to apply for the program, and when she had passed all of the tests, both physical and in demolitions school, nobody had stopped her from joining the unit.

Out on the training field, she was distracted from her plans of addressing the king when a male cadet challenged her, wanting to know if *she* could make it through the course in the allotted time. Though she thought the brat lippy for questioning her abilities, she had seen enough of the youths to know she could beat them. With the male infantry officers, it might have been different, especially for those on track for the elite forces, but these people had been chosen based on their ability to calculate math equations in the air, not because they excelled in athletics. Kaika ran side by side with her challenger for the first half of the course, her long legs taking her over the log hurdles with ease, and thanks to regular training, she had enough upper body strength to sweep her through the ropes and over the wall more quickly than he. She was waiting for him at the end when he finished, and she wriggled her fingers in invitation, to make it clear that her running the course didn't mean he got to avoid dealing with the "Cofah berserker." Aware that Zirkander and the king might be watching, she taught him a few things as they sparred instead of pummeling him straight into the ground, then sent him to the end of the line.

"Captain Kaika," Zirkander called and waved her over. He still stood at the base of the stairs alongside Angulus, looking out over the field, with two bodyguards framing them and another two on the walkway above.

Kaika jogged over, nerves plucking at her stomach. They were calling her over. Had Zirkander said something to the king? Either way, this was her chance to ask for a reassignment. She wouldn't even have to be presumptuous, not overly so, anyway.

Since she was in uniform, she saluted the king. That was a perk of military service. Civilian women traditionally genuflected, and she'd never had a stomach for bending a knee to anyone.

"Captain Kaika," Angulus said, regarding her with his dark eyes. His face did not give any of his thoughts away. "I understand you wish to speak with me."

"Yes, Sire." She opened her mouth to ask her question, but he kept speaking.

"I have several inspections and must continue on to them now." He nodded toward the walkway. "But if you report to the castle after your shift, I will see you then."

"I. Oh. Thank you, Sire."

She hadn't intended to ask him anything that would take long, and she wouldn't have minded having Zirkander nearby, if only because he might back her up, but he was already uttering a "Carry on" and heading up the stairs. He almost bumped into one of his bodyguards who didn't scurry out of the way fast enough. He growled something at the man before striding out of view.

He seemed more tense than usual, at least from the times Kaika had seen him before, and she hoped that didn't bode poorly for her meeting.

"After shift," Zirkander said. "That sounds like a dinner date. Make sure you wipe the mud off your womanly bits before you go. Angulus would be a better prize than Therrik."

Kaika almost choked on the idea of the king as a prize. She didn't consider herself shy or easily intimidated, but she would definitely feel discombobulated if she tried to woo royalty, especially royalty whose wife had been dead for less than a month.

"I'm sure neither dinner, dates, nor womanly bits are on his mind, sir."

"No? Hm." Zirkander's face had a speculative look that Kaika did not know how to interpret. "Well, I'll wish you luck with your request, and I shall leave you to your fulfilling work." He waved in parting, then headed back toward headquarters, but not before giving another long look toward the airborne fliers.

"Thank you, sir."

Kaika walked back toward the cadets, telling the nerves in her stomach that they could calm down because she wasn't going to see the king for hours. Her nerves failed to listen. They knew she would have all day to worry about what she would say to Angulus in a private audience, one that would take place in the very castle she had blown her way into three weeks earlier.

CHAPTER 2

NGULUS DUCKED HIS CHIN AS he knocked away
the jab toward his face, not trusting himself to fully stop
the quick, powerful punches of his security chief. The
man's fists were wrapped with padded gloves, but they still left
bruises when they connected.

Angulus succeeded with the block, but two more straight
punches flew toward his face, followed by an uppercut toward
his abdomen. He danced back on the balls of his feet, but not
as far as he would have liked. The ropes of the boxing square
created a barrier at his back.

When Sarkon did not press his attack immediately, Angulus
took advantage of the pause to launch an offense of his own and
sent several quick jabs toward his opponent's face. He hoped to
bring up Sarkon's arms, so he could slip a punch in from below,
but as usual, the chief's defenses were as solid as a brick wall.
Out of nowhere, padded knuckles grazed Angulus's abdomen.

He sighed and tapped his stomach to acknowledge the point.

"Had enough?" Sarkon asked, lowering his fists.

They faced each other barefoot and shirtless, sweat dripping
from both of their bodies, a testament to the hour they had spent
in the square. His face flushed from exertion, Angulus deepened
his breaths, trying to return them to a normal rhythm. He took
some pleasure in noticing that it was easier to accomplish than
it had been a few weeks ago.

"Another ten minutes," he said.

Sarkon's gray brows rose, the faded scar that notched the
corner of his left eye twitching slightly. He was almost twenty
years Angulus's senior, and had been the weapons instructor
in the castle since Angulus had been old enough to pick up his
first wooden sword, yet he was lean and wiry without any fat on

his frame. He danced circles around most people in the boxing square, even the elite soldiers stationed on the grounds. But even he appeared ready for a break. He held up a hand and grabbed one of the towels draped over the ropes.

"Is there a reason for this new dedication to fitness and boxing, Sire?" Sarkon asked.

"I've realized how much I enjoy spending time with you."

"Given how often you cursed my name in the last hour, I suspect that's a lie."

"I'm fairly certain there's a law against accusing your monarch of mendacity." Angulus grabbed the other towel and wiped his face. Yes, there was a reason he had increased his weekly hours in the gymnasium, but he didn't want to talk about it.

"If this has something to do with the kidnapping, nobody thinks poorly of you for that."

So much for not talking about it.

"Even if that's true, and I doubt it is, *I* think poorly of myself. What kind of ruler lets his *wife* drug him and hand him off to sycophants who drag him to an island where he's held prisoner for weeks?" Angulus would not confide in—or whine to—most people in the castle, but he had known Sarkon for most of his life. If his security chief ever broke confidences, Angulus hadn't caught him at it.

"A man who had no reason to believe his wife was conspiring against him."

"So a blind man. Is it better to be blind than inept?"

Sarkon grimaced. "Sire, you're not blind. And you are not the only one who was left feeling inadequate last month. I knew of her dealings with that organization, but I didn't believe she would ever be a threat to *you*. It was my fault you were captured. You should have had my head when you returned."

"Who else would box with me without pulling punches and praising my nonexistent skill?"

"Even with the limited time you have for training, you're a capable fighter."

"If that were true, I would have been able to escape that lighthouse without needing to be rescued. By the already-overly-heroic General Zirkander, no less." Angulus knew the grousing was unseemly, especially if Sarkon was feeling miserable for his own failings, but Angulus hadn't spoken to anyone of this since his return to the castle, and the words were tumbling out, needing to be spoken. Besides, Sarkon *had* asked. That would teach him.

"I thought you liked Zirkander."

"I do. Mostly." Angulus could get over the fact that the newspaper reporters treated him with much more respect than their king—after all, journalists loved stories of common men who rose to great heights—but talking to the man always left Angulus feeling wistful. What would it be like to fly off on adventures, knowing one could rely completely and utterly on one's own skills to survive? Angulus had spent his life being protected by bodyguards. He'd thought he had long since come to accept his role in the world, but these last couple of weeks, he hadn't been able to stop thinking about how he'd never had a chance to prove himself worthy of the crown that fate had handed him.

Zirkander got to prove himself—usually to public acclaim— every week. As if that weren't enough, he could chat easily and confidently with women, even a woman like Captain Kaika, someone Angulus had always felt stiff and stilted around. Of course, Zirkander wasn't the one who had been thinking fondly of Kaika ever since she had stormed into the castle, blowing up a priceless urn to show she deserved a place on a demolitions team. Fondly. He snorted at himself. That wasn't exactly the word that described his numerous dreams over the years—dreams that were bound to repeat tonight, after watching her skim through that obstacle course while humiliating young soldiers left and right. He barely remembered what he had been talking about with Zirkander, since he'd been watching her out of the corner of his eye most of the time.

Realizing Sarkon was gazing blandly at him, perhaps waiting for an addendum to that "mostly," Angulus added, "I'd just like to punch him in the face sometimes. Is that petty?"

"Extremely so, Sire."

"I thought so. That's why I haven't done it."

"Your wisdom is without bounds."

Angulus shot his old comrade a dirty look, then waved in the direction of the baths. "I have an appointment soon. Better wash up."

Beyond the gymnasium's tall windows, the cloudy afternoon sky was deepening toward twilight. As much as he wouldn't mind wandering shirtless into his meeting with Captain Kaika— preferably while flexing his muscles and looking appealingly masculine—his mother had long ago instilled rules about proper decorum into his brain. Besides, Kaika spent her days with some of the most elite soldiers in the country, soldiers who probably didn't have the layer of fat over their muscles that he had. He slowed his gait enough to eye himself in a mirror on the way to the washroom. There wasn't a *lot* of fat—in his determination not to turn into his rotund father, he'd never allowed himself to go too long without training—but he'd lost the definition he'd had when he had served as an officer in his youth. Would Kaika even find him attractive?

Seven gods, why was he thinking about this? He hurried to catch up with Sarkon.

His wife had been dead for less than a month. Even if they'd had a loveless marriage, one that hadn't involved sex in nearly ten years, the newspapers and the lords in the council would wag their eyebrows—and their lips—if he started courting a new woman. When he *did* court someone new, they would expect him to find an appropriate lady of the appropriate bloodlines, one who might give him the children that Nia never had. They certainly wouldn't approve of him courting a soldier who specialized in blowing up buildings, especially considering she had blown up part of *his* building.

Angulus couldn't help but grin at that thought. The reports had been severely garbled, and he suspected Captain Kaika herself had given him a better accounting at Zirkander's mother's house than any of his intelligence people had, but it sounded like they had arrested her and thrown her in the dungeon, only to have her blow her way out without help. Such a woman. Maybe he'd have to ignore the council and invite her to dinner. Or would dinner be too sedate for her tastes? What did a woman who handled explosives for a living do for recreation? Angulus had followed her career assiduously, but he knew little about her life or dreams outside of the reports filtered up through the chain of command.

"Sire?" came a voice from the other side of the gymnasium.

Angulus had just stepped into the hallway heading toward the baths, but he paused. That was one voice he never ignored.

"What is it, General Braksonoth?" he asked as the bespectacled, gray-haired officer jogged across the gym.

"News, Sire. Not good news. It's about—" General Braksonoth glanced at Sarkon, snapped his mouth shut, and raised his eyebrows toward Angulus.

Angulus almost waved for Braksonoth to report, since he had few secrets from his head of security, but in addition to being the battalion commander for the elite forces unit, Braksonoth monitored security for the entire nation. He received reports from intelligence officers all over the country, and his dominion went far beyond matters of the castle.

"I'll catch up with you, Sarkon," Angulus said.

"Of course, Sire."

Braksonoth waited patiently with his hands clasped behind his back until Sarkon disappeared, but his eyes burned with rare intensity.

"There's a problem at the Dandelion facility, Sire," he reported in a low voice.

"What kind of problem?" Dandelion was the code name for the biggest weapons research facility in Iskandia, an underground laboratory inside a mountain at the southern end of the Ice Blades. Few knew of its existence, except for the scientists and a handful of trusted military veterans that worked there. Angulus had almost sent Deathmaker out to join the team, and still might one day, but he would wait until the ex-pirate had proven he could be trusted to stay loyal to his new homeland.

"There was a break-in, a new tunnel bored in from the back of the facility." He frowned and shook his head slightly. "From deeper within the mountain. Two scientists were murdered in the generator room, and the radio reporting station on the side of the mountain was blown up. Our people didn't hear the noise, so we're not sure if some new kind of explosives might have been used. With the radio so close to the entrance, the soldiers that guard the ledge *should* have heard it."

Angulus gritted his teeth, more concerned about the dead men than the dead radio. He had handpicked the men for the project. He knew them all—and their families.

"Were Cofah agents responsible?" he asked.

"Colonel Troskar, the pilot who reported to me, hadn't seen sign of the enemy yet when he left. The murderers disappeared back into their tunnel and never showed themselves. Since the radio was out, Troskar left to report in right away, as he's supposed to do."

"I suspect someone blew a new entrance, elsewhere on the side of the mountain, then carved a way in. It would have been a laborious process, and it's hard to believe that our people wouldn't have heard some noise."

"Were any of the prototypes stolen?" Angulus thought of the massive rocket being built—and the incredibly powerful explosives the scientists had been testing. The three-story rocket would be difficult to walk away with, but there were other advanced weapons in there.

"According to Troskar, the enemy hadn't infiltrated the lab yet and nothing had been stolen. It might still be possible to minimize the damage. With your permission, I'd like to take a team back out there with Colonel Troskar, investigate that tunnel, and find those responsible for the murders."

"You don't have a *team* that has the clearance." Angulus could count the people who knew about the facility on his fingers and toes, and most of them were already out there. If the Cofah—or someone else—now knew about the Dandelion Project, then he had a leak somewhere. The last thing he needed was for *more* people to know about it.

"I have Colonel Troskar," Braksonoth said. "We have demolitions experts with security clearances that could be added to your list of cleared personnel. In case we *are* dealing with some new kind of explosive, it would be good to take such a soldier out there."

Demolitions expert? Angulus promptly thought of Kaika. There were others of higher rank who had her same background, but she was on the way to the castle.... He'd never brought anyone below the rank of colonel in on the Dandelion Project, but nobody could question Kaika's loyalty. And she had a high level of clearance already, thanks to her covert work in Cofahre.

Still, he couldn't deny that he was thinking of her for this because of reasons other than national security. Might this not be an excuse to get to know her without anyone nagging him about courting inappropriate people? Also, discussions held during an investigation about bombings might be less awkward and stilted than discussions held over a dinner table. Maybe he could even go along to the research facility. Then they would have *more* time to talk.

"Sire?" Braksonoth prompted.

Angulus gave himself a mental kick. Men were dead, the Cofah might have access to his prototype weapons, and all the other research in that facility could be at risk. This was *not* the time to be contemplating a woman.

"Colonel Troskar and I will both go with you," Angulus said. "I've been meaning to check up on the facility and see how the scientists are progressing." That was actually true. He had put together an *extensive* to-do list while he'd been locked in that cursed lighthouse. "We need those weapons now more than ever."

Braksonoth was staring at him. Gaping at him, actually. With his mouth hanging down to his collarbone. "Sire, this is *not* the time for you to visit. It's very likely that there are Cofah agents running around the facility, spies and saboteurs who would *love* a chance to kill the Iskandian king."

"If recent events are anything to go by, that could happen right here in this castle." Angulus frowned at the bitterness in his tone, glad Sarkon wasn't there to hear the condemnation. Why couldn't he quit obsessing about how easily his wife had arranged to imprison him?

"But, Sire, to deliberately court danger—"

"I'm not courting it. I'm going to see that this problem is resolved and that the scientists I promised would be working in a secure facility will not be in further danger. If the installation needs to be moved, I'll make that assessment when I'm there."

"I suppose we could spare a few hours to have a dirigible prepared so your security could come along, but I'd thought to fly back with Troskar right away. He came in the two-seater from the facility."

"We can still do that. General Ort is cleared to go out there. I'll get him to pilot my flier, and we'll take off as soon as Troskar and our demolitions expert are ready."

"Sire, it's foolish to go into a dangerous situation without proper security to protect you. I urge you to talk to your chief of security and have a complement of bodyguards arranged."

Seven gods, Angulus was so tired of being protected. And coddled.

"Troskar and Ort are soldiers, and we have soldiers already stationed out there. You'll be along as well, correct? I'll be surrounded by armed men. I'll take a firearm of my own, if it will make you feel better."

"It will not. Ort and Troskar are pilots; they're not trained as bodyguards."

"You're certainly capable of keeping people alive, General."

"I can't be effective at ferreting out and capturing the enemy if I'm responsible for your safety, Sire."

"Our demolitions expert will come out of the elite forces too. And your people are trained to do everything. Leave that person behind with me." That said, Angulus had no intention of telling Kaika that she would be acting as his bodyguard. She would think him helpless and inept.

Judging by the exasperated expression that Braksonoth wore, he didn't like this setup. Angulus hadn't seen the general rattled many times in his career. He wondered if he should feel special for causing such a reaction. Probably not.

"If we arrive there and it looks like more trouble than we

can handle," Angulus said, hoping to placate the general, "we'll send Ort back for reinforcements. But I'll need to think about who else I want to give clearance to. I'd prefer not to take an entire airship crew out there." The fact that there was trouble out there, when there never had been before, suggested his security measures had already failed, but he still did not want to alert more people than necessary to the Dandelion Project. The facility could be moved if necessary; the weapons *had* to remain secret, especially the rocket.

"Who are you planning to take as the demolitions expert?" Braksonoth was openly glowering now, and Angulus doubted that was the question he'd *wanted* to ask. He was probably wondering if Sarkon had knocked his king's brains out through his ears. "I would recommend Colonel—"

"I have someone in mind," Angulus caught himself saying before he thought better of it, before Braksonoth fully voiced his recommendation and Angulus had to come up with a plausible reason to object to the person. Not that kings had to come up with plausible reasons, but it seemed a good policy.

"Oh? One of my people, I presume?"

"Yes, and we'll have to take another pilot." Angulus hesitated, shuffling names through his head. "Zirkander."

Braksonoth's eyebrows shifted upward. The general had recommended they bring in Zirkander on this project no less than three times, pointing out that they needed more than two pilots who knew how to get out to the facility, especially now that Colonel Ashwonter had retired. Angulus had never been certain Zirkander had the maturity to keep secrets, but his loyalty to the country couldn't be questioned. Just so long as he didn't spend the trip trading quips with Kaika. If anyone was going to quip with her, it should be Angulus. If only he had that knack.

"Very well, Sire. How soon can you be ready?"

"Within two hours. Get Zirkander and Ort. I'll tell—"

"Sire?" a new voice called from across the gym. A young page ran in, spotted Braksonoth and halted, nearly tripping over his feet.

"Come in, Domith," Angulus said. "What is it?"

The page glanced warily at Braksonoth and spoke from across the room. "A Captain Kaika is here to see you, Sire. Alfrem said it's in your appointment book."

Nerves started sparring in his stomach. At his side, Braksonoth's eyes narrowed. Yes, he probably already knew what Angulus had in mind, and he would doubtlessly prefer someone higher ranking.

"Good," Angulus said, not looking at the general. "Have her taken to my office. I'll be there shortly."

He still smelled of the boxing ring. He needed to hurry and clean up before meeting her. If she was left in his office too long, she might poke around and find something embarrassing, like those song lyrics he'd written years before. He didn't want the first thing she learned about him to be that he'd spent his youth dreaming of running away from princely responsibilities and joining a troupe of musicians.

"Sire," Braksonoth said, his tone very careful, the kind of careful that meant he planned to oppose Angulus and was trying to frame it in a tactful manner. "Do you think—"

"Sorry, Braksonoth. We don't have time to chat. Round up our pilots. We'll meet at the landing pad in the courtyard in two hours."

"I... Yes, Sire."

As Angulus jogged toward the baths, he told himself he was simply making haste so he wouldn't have to keep a subject waiting, not because he was fleeing the general's scrutiny.

* * *

While she waited, Kaika paced back and forth on the rug in front of the king's desk, her hands clasped behind her back as she rehearsed what she would say. She had to be contrite, not cocky. And she *definitely* was not going to wink at him.

Sire, she would say, *I'm sorry about your blown-up castle and about your wife. You probably don't want to see me around the capital for a while. Perfectly understandable. Might I suggest a secret mission to Cofahre?*

"That's not cocky, right?" she muttered to herself. "I'm being considerate of his feelings."

Footsteps sounded in the hallway beyond the open door. There was a guard out there, probably stationed in that spot to ensure she didn't light anything on fire in the king's office, but this signified someone new approaching. Him.

"You can do this," she whispered as she turned toward the doorway. She pressed the heels of her freshly polished boots together and stood straight. It wouldn't hurt to be respectful while cajoling him to send her on a mission.

King Angulus strode in, but stopped a mere step into the room. He looked at her, then at his desk, then toward the corner where a dusty lute leaned against the wall. He almost seemed suspicious, as if he had expected her to be snooping. *No, Sire, I only spy on* other *country's monarchs...*

He recovered and gave her a curt nod. His hair was damp, so he must have washed recently. She hoped she hadn't interrupted him doing something important or more interesting than an audience with a soldier. He wore a thin sweater, tailored to fit him well, drawing the eye to his broad shoulders. She forced her gaze to his face instead.

"Captain Kaika," he said. "I realize there was an issue you wished to speak to me about, but something's come up."

Not again. Was he going to run off to some other meeting before she could make her request? No, he wasn't. She had to be determined. Forthright. Blunt.

"Sire, I understand you're very busy. I just wanted to know if you were irked with me because of—" She waved at the room— at the castle. "You'd have every right to be irked, and to wish to—to punish me for the part I had in that, but surely you can see that my skills are more useful out in the field."

"There's been an incident," Angulus was saying, almost speaking over her, "and we need—" He stopped and frowned. "What did you say?"

An incident? What incident? Worried she was about to sound selfish when something major was going on, she made herself finish, determined to get the words out, since that was the entire reason she had scraped buckets of mud off her body, showered, and pressed a clean uniform before coming up here.

"That if I'm being punished, there are better ways to do it than making me teach Zirkander's puppies."

Actually, there probably *weren't* better ways, but she wasn't here to be honest; she was here to get her job back.

Angulus was staring at her with a puzzled expression that she had never seen on him before. The few times they had spoken since that initial meeting, he had always appeared serious and sure of himself. The glimpse behind the kingly mask was intriguing, but she didn't want to puzzle him—she wanted to convince him to give her orders.

"I was told you were the one who arranged for my new assignment, Sire," she explained.

"Yes, because you're good, and those puppies, as you call them, are our hope for the future. I appreciate what you do in the field, but the Cofah are proving that they plan to come to *us*. And via the air. We're having more fliers built, and we need more men—more *capable* men—up there in them."

"Sire, there are lots of people who can teach the general's cadets to be capable on the ground. Bring Colonel Therrik back. He loves teaching combat and driving young officers through obstacle courses."

Angulus's expression had grown dyspeptic at Therrik's name. Perhaps she should have mentioned another officer, but Angulus trusted Therrik, didn't he? He'd been about to send him off in command of Nowon and her on that last mission.

"Since you lost your partner," Angulus said slowly, making his voice almost gentle, "and nearly your own life on your last mission, I thought you might like a break."

Kaika had not seen gentle Angulus any more often than she had seen puzzled Angulus, and she found herself flustered. She had expected to have to argue with an implacable brick wall. Instead, she was getting the man behind the crown.

"No, Sire," she said, determined not to let this change anything. "I get antsy if there's not some excitement to charge my blood. Don't know what to do with myself. Nowon kept trying to get me to take up knitting as something to do besides exercising and pacing on sea voyages, but I couldn't get through more than a row of those little yarn knots before I had the urge to turn the needles into swords and find someone to spar with."

A slight smile curved his lips. A smile was promising. And attractive. She caught herself staring at his mouth and then realized she'd lost the thread of her argument.

He sighed, and the smile faded. "I see."

She had the sense that she'd disappointed him. Because she didn't want to teach?

"Sire, *are* you angry with me? I assumed... well, I don't know. Before, when I was reporting, I know I was just giving the facts, but I am sorry about the queen. We—I—just wanted to help. I know that's not an excuse, but—"

"Captain Kaika." He lifted a hand. "I'm not angry with you." For a moment, he looked like he would continue, but he shook his head instead. "I do have something that should get your blood charged. Assuming you can leave tonight. We're taking a trip."

She blinked. A trip? Had he said *we*? Her and him? For a moment, she thought of bedroom activities, but that was ridiculous. They wouldn't need to take a *trip* for that, and he surely had no reason to think about bedroom activities with her, regardless. He must be able to find countless young and beautiful women for that.

"Sire?" she asked, hoping for clarification.

"I suppose I should ask if you're interested, rather than assuming, but this is a matter of national security, and I'm in need of your expertise."

A matter of national security? Had something happened right here on Iskandian soil? She had to keep herself from wiggling in place, eager for the news of something important and possibly dangerous that she could help with. "Yes, Sire. Of course."

"You've already taken an oath for your security clearance."

Kaika nodded. "Long ago, but I'll happily take another." Especially if it meant an exciting new assignment.

"I trust the original one will suffice," he said, some of that dryness he was known for creeping into his tone. "We're going to a secret facility that's been broken into by unidentified intruders. Explosives were used, possibly something new." His face grew more serious. "Two of our people are already dead, and we suspect enemy operatives are still in the area, perhaps planning the theft of prototype weapons."

Kaika bit her lip to keep from displaying any inappropriate expression—he'd just told her that people were dead, so she definitely should not be grinning with enthusiasm over the fact that he had chosen *her* for this mission. A secret weapons facility? She'd never heard of such a thing, which made her feel all the more honored—and excited—that he wanted to take her along.

"I'm ready, Sire," she said. "No, wait. I should grab my combat gear." And explosives of her own. She would show those intruders how to blow things up. "I can be ready in an hour, Sire."

His faint smile returned. "Good. You have an hour and a half."

"Perfect." Kaika charged for the door, nearly knocking him over, then paused with her hand on the jamb. "Er, am I dismissed?" Officers had a tendency to get in a huff when one left without waiting for an official dismissal.

He merely flicked his fingers. "Go, Captain."

CHAPTER 3

NGULUS WAITED IN THE SHADOW of his personal
flier, with General Ort at his side and his bodyguards
milling near the landing platform, looking distressed
that nobody had invited them along. Another flier waited,
already loaded with Troskar's and Braksonoth's gear. Colonel
Troskar stood by the entrance to the kitchens, explaining to the
overzealous staff that the fliers couldn't carry much weight and
they had already packed enough food to keep their king alive.
Braksonoth was on the other side of the courtyard, gesticulating
and murmuring to a colonel who would fill his boots at
headquarters until he returned.

General Ort, a steady officer nearing retirement, sent a few
covert glances at Angulus, but did not comment on what little
he'd heard about the mission thus far, including the part where
his king, in an unprecedented decision, was leaving the castle to
come along. For the most part, soldiers could be counted on to
be solid and dependable—and not to question him when he was
making questionable decisions.

The buzz of a propeller announced the arrival of the third flier
before it appeared in the night sky beyond the castle walls. Not
surprisingly, Zirkander made a flourish of his arrival, twisting
his way through a barrel roll before activating his thrusters and
landing a dozen meters to the side of the other fliers.

"If he does that while I'm in the back, I'm going to choke him
with his scarf," Angulus said. Flying made him slightly queasy,
even without acrobatics being involved. He had ridden with
Zirkander before and knew he had a tendency toward flair.
Angulus preferred sedateness.

"It's not generally a good idea to cause the pilot to pass out
when you're in the back, Sire," Ort observed. "You might simply

get revenge the same way Colonel Therrik did when flying with him."

"By letting Zirkander drug me and leave me beside the road?"

"I heard Therrik threw up before that. No pilot wants to clean vomitus out of his back seat." Ort tilted his head. "Does this mean you won't be flying with me, Sire? You could send Captain Kaika with him. I doubt crazy flying would faze her."

Angulus had considered that—Ort had been his pilot the other times they had flown out to the Dandelion facility. There was no reason not to send Kaika with Zirkander. Since he was happily involved with Sardelle, he shouldn't be working his charms on Kaika, and it wasn't as if any sort of rearranging could allow Angulus to fly with her, since neither of them was a pilot. Angulus just had this notion that Kaika would find him dull and staid after spending time with Zirkander, whereas Angulus might seem a pleasing alternative after she spent the entire ride flying with the rigidly proper General Ort.

He rubbed his face. What was he doing, worrying about something so petty? This was a mission to investigate murders and a breached top-secret facility. It wasn't a *date*.

It also wasn't fitting for him keep checking his watch and worrying that Kaika hadn't arrived yet. What if his not-a-date-but-a-demolitions-expert didn't show up? No, she would. Her record said she was dedicated and dependable, even if she shared some of Zirkander's tendencies toward flair.

Zirkander pushed his goggles up onto his forehead and hopped down from his cockpit. Ort walked over to meet him— or perhaps to *inspect* him. He frowned and eyed the younger general up and down.

Ort pointed to a creased pocket flap on Zirkander's flight jacket, then waved toward boots that were dull and smudged, especially when compared to Ort's gleaming leather footwear. "Can't you ever report to the king in a freshly pressed uniform? Did you walk through engine grease on purpose on the way out here?"

"Not on *purpose*, sir."

They might hold the same rank now, but there was little doubt as to which was the senior officer. It would probably be a while before Zirkander stopped calling Ort "sir." Still, he seemed to realize that he did not need to endure a dressing down anymore. When Ort pointed to some other deficiency on the uniform, Zirkander clapped him on the shoulder and ambled toward Angulus.

"Sire." He saluted, as was the proper protocol for a soldier in uniform. An unfortunate protocol. Angulus wouldn't have minded seeing Zirkander bend a knee. "Where're we going so late at night and without the rest of the squadron?" He peeked under Angulus's flier toward the third craft on the landing pad and nodded toward Colonel Troskar, whose face was dark with beard stubble and marked with a new gash on his forehead. He looked like he needed a bunk, rather than another flight.

"You'll find out when we get there," Angulus said, as a boy from the kitchens trotted past with bags of food and canteens of water for Zirkander's flier. Angulus wouldn't speak of their destination with so many ears around.

"Might make it hard for me to pilot us to the destination."

"Just follow Ort."

Zirkander scratched his jaw thoughtfully. His face was clean and his beard shaved, even if his uniform held a few imperfections. Reminded that he didn't want Kaika to compare him unfavorably to the pilot, Angulus wondered if it was petty to wish Zirkander had shown up dirty, scruffy, and smelly. And with a black eye. No, a black eye would be bad. A woman would be sympathetic toward such a thing and ask how it had happened. Maybe *Angulus* should get a black eye.

"General Zirkander has difficulty following," Ort said. "He likes to take the lead."

"Tough," Angulus said. He didn't see if Ort or Zirkander had a response, because the person he'd been waiting for jogged into view, trotting ahead of the guard who was clearly supposed to be escorting her around the side of the castle and to the landing pad.

Captain Kaika carried a large backpack with a tight bedroll and the tip of a rifle just visible behind her head. The pouches on her utility belt were stuffed with ammunition and who knew what else, and she also carried a heavy duffle bag under one arm. She clanked as she jogged.

"Captain," Zirkander drawled, "are we going to have a discussion about weight again?"

"You know it's dangerous to bring up weight with a woman, General." Kaika grinned at him, then saluted Angulus. "Sire."

He smiled, though the gesture felt bleak. He wanted the grin, not the salute.

Kaika's eyes were gleaming, and she looked like she was having a hard time putting that grin away. Excited by the mission, was she? He was glad he could offer it to her, but it made him feel guilty that he had given her a job staying in town and teaching. Sure, he'd had a legitimate reason, and what he told her was true, that they needed to train a new generation of pilots and increase the size and number of flier squadrons in the sky. But she was right in that many people were qualified to instruct those young officers. Angulus had wanted to have her stationed nearby, so he had time to get to know her, now that he finally could.

"Even when you're talking about her bag full of junk?" Zirkander pointed to her duffle, which, judging by all the points and lumps thrusting against the canvas sides, was full of weapons and explosives.

"*Especially* when you're talking about her junk." Kaika's grin broadened again, and she swatted herself on the butt.

"Captain *Kaika*," Ort said sternly, jerking his head toward Angulus.

Angulus barely noticed the admonition. He was too busy blushing as a flood of images involving butts and swats rushed into his mind. Thank the gods for the darkness of the courtyard; he doubted the handful of lanterns positioned around the landing pad or the soft glow from the crystals in the dragon fliers would shine light on the redness of his cheeks.

"The king was married for a long time, sir," Kaika said. "I'm sure he knows about junk." She hefted her bag. "Where can I put this?"

Zirkander pointed at his flier and opened his mouth.

Angulus cut him off before he could speak. "In General Ort's flier."

Zirkander shrugged and added, "Only *half* of it. Otherwise his flier will be scraping its belly on every tree between here and wherever we're going."

"An officer needs to be prepared for any eventuality, sir."

"You took down an entire Cofah secret laboratory with less than the enemy uniform on your back," Zirkander said. "I'm sure you can leave a few tools behind."

Ort's bushy gray eyebrows were up. They had been since Angulus had informed Kaika that she would be flying with him.

"I'd like to have a chat with Zirkander on the way out," Angulus said. "And someone in each of the fliers should know the way to the facility in case we're separated for some reason." Though he did not have to explain himself, he kept feeling compelled to, no doubt because he was thinking with his heart—or maybe a lower organ. People thinking with body parts other than their brain liked to make excuses to justify their foolishness.

Ort nodded. "Of course, Sire."

"A chat with the king?" Zirkander murmured to Ort, his voice low enough that Angulus decided to pretend he hadn't heard. "Will that be as fun for me as it sounds?"

Ort's eyes gleamed. "I hope so."

"General Braksonoth?" Kaika asked from a few feet away.

The general had finished giving his officer instructions and was heading to Troskar's flier. Kaika saluted him, but judging by the cool way he responded with, "Captain Kaika," Braksonoth wasn't pleased to see her here.

Was it just because he thought a more senior officer should go? Or did he have an inkling of what had motivated Angulus to invite her? She *was* fully qualified for this. There was no reason to be huffy over the choice.

"You're going on the mission too?" Kaika must have been aware of her C.O.'s record, but she seemed surprised to see him here. Maybe she had no idea that her bespectacled and usually mild-mannered general still did occasional fieldwork when his talents were needed.

"Yes. Stow your gear, Captain." Braksonoth dismissed her and walked toward Angulus, who braced himself for a polite, respectful, and completely unmistakable lecture.

"Sire, it's not too late. I urge you to change your mind and stay here where it's safe. Let us handle this, and then we'll report back as soon as possible. You can come out as soon as we've dealt with the threat."

Braksonoth spoke quietly, without the earlier irritation, as if he were simply making a reasonable request to a comrade. And he was being reasonable. Angulus couldn't help but feel like the unreasonable one here. He *should* stay behind, for his own safety and for the sake of the throne. The kingdom had already been disrupted once this spring. But Angulus wanted to be unreasonable for once in his adult life, to go out there and help, to show that he could. He had no intention of being a liability.

"General," he said slowly.

"We were all extremely worried when you were kidnapped, Sire," Braksonoth went on. "You know Tanders and I were stuck over in Moorage Baton and didn't get back until the trail was cold, but don't think I didn't blame myself for losing you. My people—*I*—don't want to risk losing you again."

Angulus's shoulders slumped. What could he say to that? More specifically, what could he say that didn't involve being an ass? He almost relented, agreeing to stay home for the ease of his men, but he caught Kaika and Zirkander looking in his direction. Their faces held very similar expressions, their eyes gleaming with the anticipation of adventure. Angulus should know better than to think of this mission as an adventure, especially when he knew the names of the families of the men who had died, but he couldn't help thinking of it as a chance to escape, if only for a while. He wanted to flex his muscles and to show that he was more than a signature factory for the piles of papers that crossed his desk every day.

"You won't lose me, General. You'll be right there at my side." As he clapped Braksonoth on the shoulder and headed for Zirkander's flier, Angulus did his best not to worry about the troubled expression on his general's face.

* * *

The wind whipped at Angulus's face, making him wonder why he hadn't remembered a scarf. He had flown often enough to know it was always colder in the sky than it was down below. At least Zirkander hadn't flipped them upside down yet. He was being admirably sedate as he flew behind and to the left of the lead aircraft. Ort had taken point, while Troskar and Braksonoth cruised off his other wing.

Shortly after takeoff, it had occurred to Angulus that he should have chosen to fly with Colonel Troskar. Braksonoth's second-hand report of the events in the research facility had been brief, and it would have been wise for Angulus to know about what awaited them. Instead, he had Zirkander to talk to, someone who knew even less than Angulus did. Thus far, neither of them had spoken a word, not that chatting was easy with the wind whipping past or the propeller buzzing the air. Still, Zirkander hadn't so much as glanced back. His hands remained on the flight stick, his eyes toward the sky ahead. Maybe Angulus's presence made him nervous, as hard to imagine as that was. The man never seemed nervous about anything.

"Zirkander," Angulus said, leaning forward to be heard. He had to come up with *something* to say, or the general would think it odd that they were flying together. "We're heading to a top-secret facility, one I wish to *remain* top secret. Ort and Troskar have been there before, but they're the only active-duty pilots who have. I'm trusting you to keep this secret."

For a long moment, Zirkander did not answer. He'd glanced back when Angulus had first said his name, so he must have heard. True, Angulus hadn't asked a question, but he did expect an acknowledgment.

"Sire," Zirkander finally said, peering over his shoulder. "I wish you'd asked me before assuming... Well, I mean, I *can't* keep this a secret from Sardelle."

Angulus tried to squash a flare of irritation. Was Zirkander truly saying he couldn't keep any secrets from his girlfriend? "Why not?"

The words may have come out harsher than he had intended, because Zirkander's shoulders bunched up. Hells, maybe he *was* nervous about being out here with his king, and despite his flippant attitude, maybe he cared about not annoying Angulus.

"I figured you knew, Sire," he said, sounding like he was choosing his words carefully. "Though I suppose we haven't had a frank discussion with you. But you seem to have a lot of intelligence on sorcerers and magic."

"What are you talking about?"

"Sardelle is telepathic, Sire. And, ah, so is her sword. So there will automatically be two people who know about it besides me—if you can call Jaxi a people, which I believe is what she prefers."

Now Angulus was the one who couldn't respond. Did Zirkander just call the sword a person? A *telepathic* person? Angulus had read a few old texts about magic and sorcerers, and he did recall telepathy being covered, but it hadn't occurred to him that Sardelle—and her *sword*—would have this ability.

"You, uhm, knew about Jaxi, right, Sire?" Zirkander asked.

"Just that it's the sword."

"It's a she. If you ever talk with her, she'll be quick to let you know."

"Talk with her?" Angulus had a hard time wrapping his head around the idea of a sentient sword. A female sentient sword. "In your head?"

"She'll be in *your* head. If you're a mere mortal without dragon blood, there's no way to learn telepathy, but those who have the skill can monitor our thoughts and have a conversation with us. If you're open to that, that is. My understanding is that they don't poke their noses into people's minds as a rule. Unless it's an emergency, such as when a Cofah soldier is thinking of shooting them."

Angulus stared over the side of the flier, watching the dark fields pass below as he considered this new information. The idea of someone sifting through his thoughts without him knowing it—or even *with* him knowing it—was disconcerting. And a threat to national security.

"Does this mean Sardelle knows where you're going right now?" Angulus wondered if she might already be aware of the secret facility. What if he had been thinking about it when she had been nearby? They hadn't shared space that often—she had politely declined his offer of a room in the castle, choosing to stay somewhere outside of the city—but did that mean anything? A few weeks earlier, they had been sitting close to each other at that celebratory dinner he had hosted for the pilots who had fought back the Cofah sky fortress.

"Sire, *I* don't even know where we're going."

"So, you're not communicating with her now?"

"We're outside of her range. She usually has to be close, within a mile or so to reach me. Jaxi's reach is farther, but I think we're outside of her range now too." Zirkander waved toward the dark Ice Blades looming on the horizon, the jagged peaks like a row of fangs thrusting into the starry sky. "But when we get back..." He shrugged. "I can try not to think about it, but I don't have a lot of secrets from Sardelle. Or Jaxi."

"Is that lack of privacy as uncomfortable as it sounds?" Not that Angulus had experienced much privacy in his own life—there was usually a bodyguard nearby, even when he was bathing. Still, his thoughts were his own.

"Took some getting used to, but I don't know if it makes much difference with me. I mostly say whatever's on my mind."

"I've noticed."

Zirkander did not offer a rejoinder. Angulus wagered one had come to mind, despite what he'd said. Zirkander wasn't *entirely* without tact. Most of the time. Angulus wondered what that rejoinder had been.

He could see where having a telepath at one's side would be useful—he could have known that Nia was plotting against him long before she had arranged for his kidnapping. It could be invaluable when dealing with dignitaries and representatives from other nations. Would Sardelle use her talents that way? Maybe he should take another shot at enticing her to stay at the castle. She had proven herself willing to help Iskandia, even if the nation had done nothing to help her yet.

"I should warn you that Phelistoth—the dragon—is also telepathic," Zirkander added. "In case you're ever in his range, you might not want to think about national secrets."

"Wonderful. Have you seen it at all when you've been out flying?"

"No, Sire. I've been busy generaling of late. Hasn't been much time for flying." Zirkander did not look back, but he managed to sound wistful, even with the wind eating into his words. "I've had a couple of men report spotting him, but he's being discreet. I understand that Tylie can communicate with him just about any time though. He's even visited her at the house. If you want to talk to him, you could do so through her."

Angulus had a hard time imagining a discussion of state matters and dragon-human treaties that was filtered through a sixteen-year-old girl. A *Cofah* sixteen-year-old girl at that. "She's with Sardelle? Learning magic?"

"Yes, I'm not sure that's going as well as Sardelle or Tolemek had hoped. What girl wants to learn from a human teacher when she could be riding around on the back of a dragon?"

"I honestly do not know the answer to that question."

"Apparently, the dragon is teaching her how to use her magic, but I'd prefer Tylie and *Sardelle* bond. Tolemek would have trouble leaving and going back to the empire, but Tylie hasn't blown up any airships back home. It'd certainly be helpful if she chose to stay in Iskandia, to make a life here. Also, it sounds like Tylie will be a strong sorceress someday, so we could definitely use her fighting on our side."

"We need all the help we can get," Angulus agreed, though he wasn't sure he should encourage the idea of a girl fighting for them, or for anyone at all. True, men and women could enlist in the army at seventeen, but everything he'd heard about Tylie suggested she was the mental equivalent of a twelve-year-old after the years she had lost.

"Turning south to follow the mountains," came General Ort's voice over the communication crystal embedded into the flight stick in the cockpit. Angulus barely heard the words over the wind. "Keep an eye out. Captain Kaika thought she spotted something else flying out here—four o'clock and at a higher elevation than us."

Angulus shifted in his seat, looking behind him and to the sides. Maybe he should have been watching the night sky all along. He hadn't expected to encounter other aircraft in Iskandia, but perhaps that had been a mistake. Whoever those spies were, they had reached the inland Dandelion facility somehow, and it wasn't the most accessible place.

After taking a look at the sky all around them, Zirkander tapped the communication crystal. "This is General Zirkander, Wolf Squadron," he said, broadcasting wide. "If there's another pilot out here snuggling up to the Ice Blades, identify yourself."

All of the military craft had communication crystals now, and Angulus held his breath, waiting to hear if Zirkander would receive a response. There were some decommissioned and older model fliers that had gone into private collections before crystals had been installed, but he doubted barnstormers would be flying around at midnight.

"No response?" Angulus asked.

He didn't know how the new crystals worked or what their range was, only that Sardelle had built them using her magic. *That* information had only come to light recently. Zirkander had originally convinced General Ort to have them installed, proclaiming they were some ancient artifacts that he'd found, and that if they were magic, he had no knowledge of it. Because they'd been so useful, people who feared magic had looked the other way and not asked too many questions, much as they didn't openly question where the larger crystals that acted as power sources for the fliers had come from.

"Nothing, Sire," Zirkander said.

"Hood your crystals," General Ort said when nobody responded. "We'll continue on course, unless His Highness objects, but we'll watch the skies."

Angulus nodded when Zirkander looked back. He didn't want to risk showing more people to the facility, but until someone saw something more definitive, he didn't want to risk a delay, either. He vowed to keep an eye out himself.

Zirkander pushed the hood over his crystal, and the soft light that it emitted disappeared. Angulus could barely see the cockpit in front of him. He couldn't see Ort's or Troskar's fliers at all and wondered how Zirkander knew where to go. It was hard to hear the other craft over the sound of their own propeller.

They flew along in silence for a few more minutes, and none of the pilots reported seeing anything. Perhaps Kaika had been mistaken, or simply glimpsed some raptor out to hunt at night.

"Do you believe Sardelle will keep the information about the facility secret?" Angulus asked, though he suspected he already knew the answer. From the few conversations he'd had with her, she did not seem to be someone who would run around town, getting drunk and spilling secrets. She always came across as quiet and serene, something she had managed even when reporting on a powerful enemy sorceress approaching on a floating fortress.

"Absolutely," Zirkander said without hesitation.

"And the sword?"

This time, Zirkander *did* hesitate. Angulus arched his eyebrows.

"Well, she doesn't talk to that many people, Sire. Most Iskandians wouldn't believe that she exists, even if she spoke into their minds. My mother, for example, doesn't believe in witches, sentient swords, or anything to do with magic."

"So she doesn't know that Sardelle…"

"No, Sire."

For a moment, Angulus was tickled by the idea of Mrs. Zirkander not knowing that her son's lover was a sorceress. But he couldn't let himself be distracted from a question that involved national security.

"Was that your way of saying the sword *can't* be trusted to keep secrets?" Angulus asked. "Very few people know about this installation, Zirkander. We have advanced weapons research and experimentation going on."

This was the Iskandian equivalent to the Cofah volcano

base that Zirkander's people had blown up, if on a smaller scale. Angulus's scientists didn't have dragon blood to power their weapons, but they were doing impressive work with rockets. Enough, he hoped, to keep the Cofah away from their coasts in the future.

"Oh, she's trustworthy, Sire. It's just that she's also, uhm, blunt. She speaks her mind. Whether you want her to or not. But I don't think this will be a problem. As far as I know, she only talks to Sardelle and occasionally to me and Tolemek."

"*Tolemek?*" Angulus asked, a surge of alarm flooding his veins. He might have thought of one day adding the ex-pirate and ex-Cofah subject to the scientists working on the weapons, but he'd assumed that would be years in the future, after Tolemek had proven that he was done with his empire and would never think of betraying Iskandia. He'd only been here for a few months. It was too soon to know his true mind.

"Yes, because he has dragon blood, too, and she needed to help him back when Tolemek was keeping those pirates from blowing up the city." Zirkander frowned over his shoulder toward the sky between the fliers and the mountains. When he went on, he sounded distracted. "Once Jaxi's been in your mind, she tends to assume you're friends and stick around. I'm positive she'll talk to you when we get back if you ask Sardelle about it. Though I should warn you..." Zirkander shook his head and faced forward again. "She has no problem offering opinions on your love life while she's sauntering through your thoughts."

Angulus was looking toward the mountains, wondering if Zirkander had seen something, but he frowned back at him. "My love life? There's not much to talk about there."

"Yes, Sire."

Angulus frowned. That *Yes, Sire* had sounded very careful. What did Zirkander think he knew?

"She actually wanted me to tell you—ah, never mind." Zirkander coughed and stared intently forward.

"What?"

"Nothing, Sire. I shouldn't have said anything."

Angulus considered dropping it—surely, they had more

important things to dwell upon. But the idea that a sentient and telepathic sword had been monitoring him in some way disturbed him. He wanted to know if he had anything to worry about.

"I could give you a royal command and demand that you tell me," Angulus said.

Zirkander slumped low in his cockpit, his shoulders sinking in defeat. "Are you doing that, Sire?"

Angulus sighed. If the man truly didn't want to share, he shouldn't make him. "No."

Before he could decide if he wanted to continue the conversation, a shot rang out.

Zirkander sat up straight and looked in all directions. It hadn't sounded that close, but Angulus did not think it had come from the dark foothills far below. He had heard it clearly over the buzz of the propellers.

"Who was that?" came Colonel Troskar's voice over the crystal.

"I don't know," Ort growled, "but there's a new bullet hole in the side of my flier."

"Evasive maneuvers," Zirkander said, taking them up and tilting them sideways so sharply that Angulus would have fallen out if he hadn't been buckled in.

"I don't see anyone," Troskar said.

"You can count on him being behind us," Zirkander said, taking them upside down as he now directed the flier back in the direction they had originally come from.

Though his heart was in his throat—more from the crazy flying than from being shot at—Angulus told himself that the harness would keep him secure. He clenched his legs around his pack, less certain about the security of the gear, and grabbed his rifle. He had to unbuckle it to get it out, and he stared up—or rather *down*—as they flew, trying to spot whoever had shot at them. Or more specifically, whoever had shot at Ort's flier. Had the person expected Angulus to be with Ort? Or was he simply targeting the closest craft?

Zirkander ended his long loop, coming down far behind

Troskar and Ort, who had parted ways and flown to the sides. He raked the dark sky with bullets, every fourth or fifth one an incendiary round that lit up the night with a streak of orange. If the ammunition hit anything, Angulus couldn't tell. It would be the wildest luck, since they still couldn't see anything.

"I was hit again," Ort said. "From behind, I think. Stay down, Kaika."

Her reply, though hard to hear since the crystal was in the cockpit, sounded something like, "To all the hells with that idea."

Angulus winced. He knew she was a soldier, but he hated the idea of her being shot out here by some hidden sniper, especially if that sniper was expecting Angulus.

He raised his rifle, but he had no idea where to shoot. Zirkander was weaving and looping, trying different angles and planes as he fired experimentally into the dark night. Angulus's stomach lurched with each gravity-defying movement.

"You're wasting ammo, Ridge," Troskar said.

"Only if I don't hit someone. And that's General Ridge to you, Chast. Didn't you see my new hat?" Zirkander sounded excited by this action. He swooped again, this time turning them sideways as he angled up toward the stars.

"I did, but I was certain you'd stolen it from a secondhand store. That promotion can't be real."

They *both* sounded excited. Angulus had never even heard stolid and silent Colonel Troskar make a joke before now.

"Well, it's always possible I'll be demoted if I make the king throw up," Zirkander said.

Angulus's stomach protested another quick turn that nearly tilted them upside down again.

"Cut the chatter," Ort said. "I just heard another shot. They're definitely targeting me."

"No," Troskar said. "They're targeting all of us. A bullet almost took my scarf off a second ago."

"More than one shooter," Zirkander said. "They're being careful with their ammo. Either that, or someone's using a sniper rifle instead of a machine gun."

"Is it possible someone is shooting at us from the

mountainside?" Angulus eyed the dark crags they had been following. They seemed too far away, especially if they were dealing with a stationary sniper with a single rifle, but he had a hard time judging distance with the flier gyrating like a drunken dancer. He bit his lip to keep from asking if the military actually *paid* Zirkander to do this. He was probably keeping them alive. *This* flier hadn't been hit yet.

"Too far away," Zirkander said. "And we're five miles past the original spot now, even with our loops."

How could he know? All Angulus saw were stars and dark blurs of mountains and land, depending on how upside down they were at any given moment.

"Hah," Zirkander barked.

It took Angulus a second to see why. A small starburst of flames was burning. In the middle of the sky.

"What the—" he started to ask, but Zirkander unloaded rounds toward that spot.

Angulus's ears couldn't tell him if they struck anything, but then he saw another burst of flames, one of the incendiary bullets igniting something flammable. The scent of smoke tickled his nostrils, overpowering the gunpowder he could smell from their flier's machine guns.

"See that smoke?" Zirkander asked. "Target it. We've got two fliers out here. Invisible."

"Anyone want to tell me how that's possible?" Ort growled, coming around.

"I'd be happy to discuss it in detail once the fight's over, but I'm going to say magic right now."

Their flier was about to pass the spot where Angulus had seen the flames. Zirkander was already banking to come back around and take another run at the invisible craft, but Angulus leaned over the side with his rifle. The flames had already burned out, and he couldn't see much smoke in the darkness, but they were close enough that he was positive he could hear another propeller. He took his best guess and fired three times before they went too far for him to target the spot.

He did not expect to hit anything, or to be aware of it if he *did* hit something, but a man screamed, startling him.

"Nice shot, Sire," Zirkander said, his voice subdued for the first time since the skirmish had begun, maybe because he was offering congratulations on possibly killing a man.

Angulus didn't know how he felt about that himself. He had served in the military for several years in his early twenties, but nobody had ever entertained the notion of sending him out to Cofahre on a ship or dirigible, or even letting his unit wander off anywhere it might see real action. He'd signed plenty of orders that had condemned people to death, on both sides of the war, but he had never shot anyone.

"That one's going down," Zirkander announced. Angulus couldn't guess how he knew for certain. "But there's a second one out here. Don't get cocky." He muttered something else, the words too low for Angulus to pick up, but he thought he caught Sardelle's name. Wishing they had some magic of their own out here?

Angulus wouldn't have minded it, either. The idea of enemy aircraft more than a hundred miles inland was disturbing but not without precedent. Enemy *magic* was another matter.

"Nobody's cockier than you, Ridge," Troskar said. "We—"

A flaming orange ball the size of a steam wagon shot up from the ground, illuminating the night sky all around it. Before Angulus could start to guess how it had come to be and what it meant, it slammed into the belly of Colonel Troskar's flier. Wood and bronze exploded like a bomb.

Angulus was so startled that his rifle almost tumbled free from his fingers. All he could do was gape at the sky where the other flier had been. Nothing but ash remained, clouding the air still burning from the fireball's passing. No, there was one other thing that remained: the glowing yellow power crystal. Melted free from its casing, it fell a mile before disappearing into the trees far below.

Still gaping, Angulus watched its path. His mind refused to work, refused to grasp what had happened. Colonel Troskar and General Braksonoth had been there one second, and now were gone. Incinerated.

"Get me closer," came Kaika's shout through Ort's communication crystal.

"No." Ort sounded as dazed as Angulus felt. "We have to get the king out of here. This is—"

"Throw it, Kaika," Zirkander ordered, his voice calm, devoid of all emotion now.

Angulus groped to find calm of his own, to kick his brain into function. He had handled emergencies before, but always from the detached safety of the castle, not from five thousand feet in the air while weaving and darting through the sky like a drunken hummingbird. And not while being fired at by... a sorcerer. Or sorceress. That was what it had to be. He remembered seeing fireballs being hurled at the fliers attacking the sky fortress, but they had been tiny blazes of light from his vantage point on the ground. This was—

"Three bombs away," Kaika announced. "Tried to aim them toward wherever she is. Let's see how well she attacks us with trees falling on her."

"She?" Ort asked.

"Just assuming it's the bitch from the fortress."

"Look out, Ridge!" Ort yelled at the same time as Angulus was hurled sideways.

Once again, he would have been flung from the flier if not for his harness. How he managed to keep hold of his rifle, he didn't know, but he clenched it—and the side of the seat well—as if his life depended on it.

The sky lit up from below, another orange fireball streaking upward—straight toward them. Zirkander had them flying on their side, veering away from it, but it moved as fast as a cannonball. It grew in Angulus's vision, and it was even larger than he had realized. More like the size of a house than a wagon. He felt the heat, heard the crackling of the flames. The orange light, writhing like fire in an oven, grew so intense that he had to squint his eyes shut, waiting for it to engulf him, for his life to end in pain.

Instead, the fireball raced past five meters away. The heat was enough to sear Angulus's face, but it didn't damage him or

Zirkander's dancing flier.

Faint booms sounded from below. Angulus forced himself to tear his gaze from the fireball as it continued to streak toward the stars. He looked down in time to watch one of Kaika's bombs lighting up the dark forest. From this height, he had no idea if the explosives had hit anywhere near the person throwing those fireballs. Would it matter, even if they had? Angulus knew that Sardelle could shield herself from bullets. Wouldn't this other sorceress be able to do the same?

"Keep an eye out," Zirkander said. "It's not tough to dodge those fireballs if you see them coming." His voice dropped to a barely audible mutter. "Not that that helps Chast."

"We're getting out of here before she throws more," Ort said. "Head south, Ridge."

"Wait. There's the other flier. A two-seater, just one pilot. He's visible now. Your three o'clock." The flier engine surged as Zirkander headed in that direction, the dark silhouette of the mountain range looming ahead.

"I'll get him," Ort said. "Get the king out of here, away from that witch and away from anything else."

Zirkander did not respond to the command. He arrowed straight toward the mountains.

There was no telltale glow of an energy crystal—the dragon blood that powered the Cofah aircraft was more subtle—but Angulus could finally see the outline of the other craft, now that they were pointed straight at it. Zirkander flew toward it relentlessly, like a charging boar.

Angulus did not object. He didn't want to flee like a coward. He raised his rifle, hoping he would get a chance to shoot the pilot, to kill the people responsible for Braksonoth's and Troskar's deaths.

"Zirkander," Ort barked.

Like a hound that had sighted its prey, Zirkander didn't seem to hear the warning. He opened up with the machine guns, hammering rounds toward the other flier as they came in from behind and to the side.

The other pilot must have still believed he was invisible.

Only when bullets streaked toward him did he start evasive maneuvers. He banked and flew closer toward the mountains while sweeping back and forth like a pendulum on a horizontal plane.

Zirkander, heading straight after him, closed ground quickly. Angulus kept his rifle ready, wanting that shot, but he would have had to shoot over Zirkander's head, and that would have meant unbuckling himself so he could rise up in his seat. Given the general's propensity for flipping upside down, that seemed unwise.

Besides, his rifle skills weren't necessary. Zirkander anticipated the pilot's path—the Cofah's maneuvers weren't nearly as gravity-defying as his—and caught him, tearing off the flier's tail with his barrage of bullets.

The Cofah lost control immediately. He was probably doomed by then, but Zirkander stuck with him and continued to fire. The pilot slumped over in his seat. The nose of the Cofah craft dipped down, and it streaked toward the mountainside with smoke and flame flowing from its fuselage. In seconds, it crashed into the rocky ground, scattering pieces of the burning flier across the slope.

Only when Zirkander pulled up did Angulus realize how close their momentum had taken them to striking the mountain. For a moment, that fate seemed inevitable, as their belly nearly brushed boulders and shrubs before the engine overcame gravity and they soared toward the stars again.

For the first time since the battle had begun, Zirkander looked back at Angulus. "You all right, Sire?"

"I'm... uninjured." *All right* was another matter. Angulus looked back toward where those fireballs had come from, toward where General Braksonoth had been incinerated. Braksonoth had worried about *him* being killed out here. It hadn't occurred to either of them that he would be the one to die so quickly, so meaninglessly. As Angulus's breaths returned to normal and his nerves settled, he could already feel the weight of responsibility— and regret—smothering him like a wet blanket. "Let's get out of here."

CHAPTER 4

KAIKA DROPPED HER BACKPACK AND duffle bag to the ground and climbed out after them. General Zirkander and the king had landed first on the flat ledge, and they had already left their fliers. Nobody was talking yet. If the others were as stunned by the loss of General Braksonoth and his pilot, she could understand why. The air battle was only twenty minutes in the past. They had flown another fifteen or twenty miles and arrived at their destination. Wherever that was.

She tried to make herself look around and check for enemies, rather than dwelling on Braksonoth's death, but that was hard. She couldn't believe someone with such a long and accomplished record in the elite forces could disappear just like that. It wasn't fair. He should have been given a chance to fight. If Kaika saw that damned sorceress, she was going to find a way to blow her into the farthest reaches of the deepest hell.

She ground her teeth as she stalked about, examining their ledge. As far as she could tell, which wasn't very far thanks to the darkness, they were halfway up the side of a mountain toward the southern end of the Ice Blades. A cliff rose up to one side, one that didn't seem to hold any caves or other openings, at least none that were visible in the night. On the other side of the ledge, which would have been large enough for a couple of modest houses to perch upon, the ground dropped away. It wasn't a sheer drop, and Kaika had spotted a trail carving its way down the steep slope as they had landed. Trees rose up, perhaps three hundred feet below, and a coyote yipped somewhere in the forest. A pile of camouflage netting lay on one end of the ledge, but whatever it usually guarded wasn't there now.

Ort was the last one to climb out of the fliers, his boots hitting the ground at the same time as Zirkander lit a lantern, the soft flame flaring to life. The king was already heading toward the cliff, as if he expected to find something there. A secret entrance? There must be. Nobody had mentioned an emergency landing, so this must be their destination.

Ort stalked toward Zirkander, his fists clenched at his sides.

"I gave you an order," Ort growled, then surprised Kaika by grabbing Zirkander by the front of his jacket. She didn't know the stolid general that well, but she had never seen Ort anything but calm, almost to the point of blandness. Now his face, visible by the lantern light, was flushed red.

Zirkander didn't look surprised. He merely stood there as Ort gripped his jacket, his knuckles tight against his skin.

"I *told* you to get the king out of danger, and you went after that other flier," Ort said. "Did you think that was one of your soldiers behind you, someone trained to die fighting if necessary?"

"No, sir," Zirkander said, his tone more sedate than usual. "But he seemed to be enjoying himself. He shot a Cofah pilot."

"*Enjoying* himself?" Ort glanced toward the king, who was touching the rock wall beyond the influence of the lantern's light. "He just lost General Braksonoth. And we lost Chast, damn it." Emotion thickened Ort's voice, regret now mixing with the anger.

"I know that, sir."

Kaika shifted her feet, uncomfortable watching the exchange. As Ort continued to chastise Zirkander, she plucked her rifle from her gear and walked the perimeter of the ledge. She peered into the darkness below more closely this time, searching for light or any sign that more trouble might be out there. Like that sorceress. Kaika couldn't know for certain that it was the same person that she, Sardelle, and Tolemek had fought in the bowels of the sky fortress, but her gut told her it was. She had seen those fireballs before.

Aside from the coyotes, the forest was still, with no sign of humanity for as far as the eye could see. She walked over to join the king, who had now taken out a lantern of his own. He was still touching the cliff, a different spot now.

He looked at her. "There's a rock that protrudes that you can twist. Somewhere around here. I've never been out here in the dark before."

He sounded apologetic that he couldn't wave his hand and open whatever secret door it was they were looking for. He appeared uninjured and none the worse for the battle, but he was wearing his royal mask, his thoughts impossible to discern. Braksonoth was someone who had reported directly to the castle at times. Angulus might have known the general better than Kaika had. He'd been responsible for her missions for the last few years, but they had never interacted outside of work. She'd rarely been back in the rear long enough to get to know any of her senior officers well. Still, she knew Braksonoth's expertise had been vital to their military and his death was a tremendous loss to the kingdom.

"Sorry we lost the other team, Sire," Kaika said. She was awful at condolences, but felt she should try. Maybe it would matter to him.

"So am I," he said quietly and returned to grabbing rocks.

Kaika shouldered her rifle and joined him. The cliff was cool under her hands and damp from a recent rain. She tried to find protruding rocks by the dim light of the lantern, then looked toward the ground, wondering if there might be a path worn in the stone.

She spotted something light colored against the dark rock a few feet away and walked over to look more closely. It turned out to be a small strip of clothing caught in a crack in the rock. A piece of someone's shirt torn free in a rush? She rubbed it between her fingers. Or maybe part of a dress. There was a hem on one side, and it wasn't sturdy fabric, nothing like a military uniform.

"Are there women out here, Sire?"

Angulus joined her. "Two of the scientists are women, yes."

"This isn't wet." Kaika held the scrap out to him. "When did it rain? This morning, right? Then it cleared up this evening. At least back home." She eyed the damp rocks, guessing the weather had been about the same here.

"You think whoever's garment this was went in or left after the rain? That probably means it would have been after Colonel Troskar left the facility and flew home to warn us." Angulus frowned at the rock wall. "That doesn't make sense. The murders had already happened by then. If anything, the soldiers and scientists should have stayed inside. Well, maybe not. Braksonoth said the threat originally *came* from inside. Something about a tunnel." He thumped his fist on the wall. "I should've spent more time with Troskar, gotten more information from him, and from Braksonoth. Now it's too late."

His mask was fading again, a hint of anguish slipping through. Kaika's instincts were to back away and let him be alone, the same as she had with Ort and Zirkander, but she laid a hand on his arm instead. He had lost his wife in the last month and now someone he'd worked with for years, if not decades.

"We'll figure it out, Sire. Zirkander's good, and so am I." All right, Zirkander was good in the *sky*, and investigating mysteries and murders wasn't exactly her job, but she had worked through a few puzzles in her day. True, Nowon had been the one to figure most of those out, but if examining some explosion site was key here, she could definitely do that.

Angulus looked down at her hand on his arm, and she withdrew it, suddenly feeling presumptuous. He wasn't some colleague; he was her king. Was there a rule about commoners touching royalty? Even if the lines weren't as strict as they had been in centuries past, there probably was.

"Thank you, Kaika." He tilted his head as he met her eyes. "Or do you prefer Astuawilda?"

"I prefer to shoot people who call me that," she said, wincing at the sound of the terrible syllables. "But since you've already been shot at tonight, I'll just politely inform you of my preferences." She realized she was being presumptuous again—or had that been a threat? Was it her fault that he seemed like a colleague rather than a monarch right now, dressed in plain travel clothing with his sweat-dampened hair sticking up in numerous directions? "Sire," she added belatedly.

He didn't seem to notice her irreverence, or the threat.

"Technically, I don't think our flier was shot at. We just had a fireball flung in our direction. Of course, my eyebrows *were* nearly seared off."

"That's probably a suitable punishment for using my first name." She winked before she caught herself. What was she doing? Flirting?

His eyebrows twitched upward.

"Uhm." Kaika cleared her throat and studied the cliff wall. "That protruding rock must be around here, huh?"

"Yes." Angulus reached over her head and twisted a rounded rock. "Step back."

A thunk sounded, followed by a scraping noise, and a clink-clink-clink of a chain unwinding. Kaika scooted to the side as a rectangular section of rock swung outward. It was large and heavy, revealing a cement tunnel wide enough to drive a steam carriage through. The passage was unexpectedly well lit. Lamps dangled from the ceiling at regular intervals, metal cages surrounding light bulbs. Electricity was still new in the capital, and Kaika had only seen such lamps a few times. There had been talk about getting wiring run to the military forts and flier hangars, but nothing had come of it yet. She certainly hadn't expected some cave in the middle of nowhere to be so equipped.

"Sire," General Ort said, jogging over to join them. "As the ranking officer here, I feel it's my responsibility to keep you safe. Given that there are no troops stationed at their posts—" he waved to the ledge and also to the tunnel, which was empty of everything except those lamps, "—as I was led to believe there would be, we should return to the capital immediately. It's not safe for you to be here."

Zirkander walked up, his hands stuffed in his pockets. He wore a rifle across his back, but he hadn't yet unpacked his flier.

Angulus looked at him. "Is that what you think, too, Zirkander?"

"I think I'm curious and would like to explore that tunnel, Sire."

Ort glowered at him, his boot shifting, as if to kick his colleague in the shin. His expression never changing, Zirkander lifted his boot and set his foot down outside of Ort's reach.

"But I do agree with General Ort insofar as your safety is concerned," Zirkander added. "I can take you back. Ort and Kaika can look around, or they can come back too. Whatever you think is best. We'll get Sardelle and maybe Tolemek if you're willing to bring him out here. Then we can come back better equipped to deal with that sorceress." He grimaced.

Sardelle had said the other sorceress, somehow woken from a centuries' long sleep, was far more powerful than she was. It had taken Sardelle *and* Tolemek to distract her while Kaika set explosives in that flying fortress. And distract her was *all* they had done; neither of them had come close to killing the woman.

Angulus looked at Kaika. Was he asking for all of their opinions? Since she was just a captain, she was surprised he would care what she thought.

"Whatever you want to do, Sire," she said. "I'm with you."

She hoped that being *with him* wouldn't involve her being sent home. That empty tunnel beckoned to her, promising a mystery and maybe some danger inside. Hadn't he said something about spies and strange explosives? She could barely keep from trotting inside to explore on her own.

"Good," Angulus murmured softly, the words seemingly just for her. He smiled slightly before turning back toward the generals. "We might be in danger all over again if we fly back. We have to assume the sorceress is still alive, and she may have more people with fliers out there. She might be able to track us down again, perhaps by the magic in the energy crystals powering our craft."

Ort blinked. He might not have considered that they had been tracked. Zirkander nodded grimly, not appearing surprised.

"Also, I have people in here," Angulus went on, tilting his head toward the tunnel, "people I hand-selected for this project. People who were led to believe that this was a secret facility and that they would be safe, no matter what kind of work they produced. At least two of those people are dead." He frowned down at his hand, rubbing the piece of fabric between his fingers. "And I'm afraid there's been more trouble since Troskar left to report that. I'm going to take a look."

"Sire," Ort started to protest.

Angulus stopped him with an upraised hand. "I agree that we need help. I want you to go back to the capital, Ort. Find Sardelle. You'll bring her out here personally and anyone she thinks could be useful in dealing with the situation." He frowned again. Not certain about Tolemek? "I also want you to tell Colonel Porthlok from Intelligence. He knows about this place. Have him pick a few solid men and bring them out. In fliers. I don't want an entire dirigible crew to know about the facility."

"Duck, Crash, and Colonel Sankoft from Tiger Squadron would be good," Zirkander said. "Duck was with us on the Cofahre mission and knows quite a few secrets already. The others are trustworthy."

"Tenderfoot and Vart from my company would be good for tunnels," Kaika offered, not sure whether her suggestions for personnel would be considered here.

"You heard them, Ort," Angulus said. "Hurry, and get back out here."

"Sire." Ort removed his cap and pushed sweaty hair back from his forehead. "I agree that there are still threats that we might run into if we fly back, but leaving you here without any guards..."

Kaika frowned. She wasn't a bodyguard, but she could keep Angulus alive unless they faced truly overwhelming odds. "I can watch the king's back, sir."

Ort's expression only grew bleaker. She tried to tell herself that he had never seen her shoot or fight and didn't know that she was damned good at her job, but it didn't work. She found her lips curling back in a challenge.

Zirkander slapped her on the back. "We both will. Only Kaika will do it effectively. Look, General, if you hurry, you can be back shortly after dawn. Five hours round-trip, and it won't take long to get everyone. Sardelle's in my new cottage outside of the city, the one that hasn't been blown up yet. I figure fate is waiting until I've selected a new couch and really settled in to let that happen."

Zirkander offered a smile, but neither Angulus nor Ort was looking at him, nor were they looking at Kaika. They were staring at each other, Angulus appearing stubborn and annoyed, and Ort appearing very similar.

"It's not open for discussion, General," Angulus said. He did relent and add, "We won't go far. You've been into the testing chamber and seen the labs. It's a defensible area. We'll wait there for you to return with more troops."

"Defensible against normal people, maybe," Ort said. "What if that sorceress shows up here?"

"We left her twenty miles back. Unless she has a flier waiting for her, she won't make it here before you get back, assuming you leave soon."

"She might *have* a flier." Ort sighed, but finally dipped his head in acceptance. "Stay safe, my liege." Though propriety only demanded a salute, he dropped to one knee and touched his forehead before rising and walking stiffly toward his craft. "Ridge, see me to my flier."

It seemed a strange request, since his flier was less than ten meters away, but Zirkander walked after him without comment. Angulus pocketed the fabric and took a couple of steps into the tunnel.

Kaika started after him, but paused, catching Ort's whispered words, words that clearly weren't meant for her—or the king—to overhear.

"What do you think about knocking him out, tying him up, and throwing him in the back of one of our fliers?" Ort asked. "It's for his own good. It's ludicrous for him to be out here."

Zirkander shook his head. "I think we'd both lose our heads if we succeeded."

"He wouldn't kill us for trying to save his life. I don't think."

"Our careers, then." Zirkander's hand lifted toward his flier, as if to reach out and stroke it.

"Damn it, Ridge. You can't put your career ahead of the king's life. It's our duty to keep him alive."

"It's our *duty* to follow his orders. Besides, who's going to knock him out? Unless you're a better pugilist than I remember,

I'd be the scapegoat, and he's got forty pounds on me."

"Together we could—"

Aware of movement inside the tunnel, Kaika only had time to step back before Angulus stormed past her. Judging by the livid expression on his face, he'd heard at least some of that conversation.

"If *either* of you lays a finger on me, I'll have *both* of your heads," Angulus roared, his anger surprising Kaika, more because she had never seen him lose his temper than because it wasn't justified.

Ort's shoulders slumped. Zirkander's face paled. Kaika had never seen him wearing such a distressed expression, not even in the face of certain death, but having his king angry with him clearly drove horror into his heart. He lifted his hands, looking very much like someone who wanted to deny all culpability, but he kept his mouth shut.

"Ort, get in your flier and get back to the city and follow my orders before I shove you off that ledge."

"Yes, Sire." Ort ducked his chin, then scrambled into the cockpit as quickly as any young cadet.

"Be careful out there, sir," Zirkander said and stepped away from the flier.

Already activating the thrusters, his back stiff and his face unreadable, Ort did not look down or acknowledge the warning.

Angulus looked at Kaika. She straightened her back, hoping he wouldn't think she'd had anything to do with the conversation. She could sympathize with the generals' desires to keep the king safe, but she couldn't see laying a hand on Angulus, unless it was to shove him out of the way of an oncoming bullet.

Fortunately, his fury did not appear to be for her. When their eyes met, he winced, his expression shifting from anger to apology, as if he was embarrassed to have been caught yelling.

"Zirkander," Angulus said as Ort lifted off, "toss that camo netting over your flier, then follow us inside."

"Yes, Sire," Zirkander said, his voice contrite. From him, that tone was even rarer than the king's fury.

"Kaika?" Angulus removed his rifle from his back and held it in his arms. "Let's go."

As he headed into the tunnel, Kaika hurried to catch up. She strode at his side, so she could see the way ahead, and so that she could spin and protect his back if needed. More than ever, she felt the need to ensure he walked out of here safely. As serious as this mission was, her body hummed with excitement. She had wanted a worthwhile assignment, and now she had it.

CHAPTER 5

K AIKA STEPPED OUT OF THE tunnel and into the hollowed-out chamber ahead of the king, her rifle ready as she searched every dark nook and corner with her eyes. For the moment, she paid little attention to the three-story cylindrical construct of conduits and panels in the center, or to the smaller, unfamiliar mechanical contraptions that rested on the floor in the back, or to the glass-walled laboratories lining one side of the cavernous chamber. Instead, she searched for signs of danger, eyes alert to movement, her ears straining to detect sounds, her nose inhaling the strange mix of scents inside. Chemicals, moisture, and something akin to burned black powder. A faint hum came from a distant wall, or perhaps another level of the complex, and the floor vibrated faintly.

She did not see anyone crouched in the shadows, either in the chamber or in the labs, but she spotted and pointed at two unmoving men in blood-stained white lab coats, their bodies laid out on the cement floor alongside a wall. Even from several meters away, she could tell from their frozen faces and pale features that they were dead. Their hands rested across their abdomens, and duffle bags lay at their feet.

"Rigger and Korawhacten," Angulus said quietly. "The two scientists I was told about." He stepped up beside Kaika, eyeing a ceiling so high that the light did not reach it, and then the labs, their clutter-filled interiors visible through the glass walls. "But where's everyone else? There should be eight other scientists and six soldiers here."

"Hiding?" Zirkander suggested from behind them.

"From the king's wrath?" Kaika asked, doing another survey of the chamber as they spoke. Her instincts itched, telling her that danger awaited them here.

Angulus shook his head, apparently not finding her joke funny. Not surprising, since he had just displayed that wrath a few minutes ago. Besides, this wasn't the time for jokes. She clamped her mouth shut and told herself to talk only when spoken to, or when she had something useful to volunteer.

She wanted to walk the perimeter and check more closely for people, but she did not want to leave the king's side, especially after she had promised Ort she would take care of him. She trusted Zirkander's unparalleled combat skills in the sky, but she was the better person to act as a bodyguard on the ground.

"I meant that they might be hiding from whatever killed those men." Zirkander didn't seem to be in the mood for humor, either. He nodded toward the bodies.

"*This* would be the logical place to hide," Angulus said. "That glass would let them see out of their labs, but it's so thick that it's bulletproof. It was designed to withstand a lot of force, in the event of accidents." He tilted his head toward the enormous cylindrical construct. Whatever it was, he had more of a clue than Kaika. "Anyone see any tunnels in here? Besides that one over there? That goes up to the sleeping quarters and down to the generator room. Troskar mentioned a tunnel that someone burrowed into the facility. Also that the intruders might have blown their way into the mountain from somewhere else."

"I didn't see a gaping hole in the cliffs during our approach," Zirkander said, "but I could have missed it in the dark."

Angulus grunted. "I don't think your eyes miss much, General, not when you're flying." The words, as much a compliment as statement of fact, seemed an apology of sorts. Maybe he felt bad about yelling, or maybe he realized Zirkander hadn't been the one spearheading that conversation.

Zirkander barely seemed to notice the words, but Kaika found herself wishing Angulus had a compliment for *her*. She hoped she would have a chance to prove her own capabilities to the king out here. He must have seen reports of some of her missions over the years—even though she was a mere captain, she and Nowon had done some militarily and nationally important work in Cofahre, especially of late. But he had never seen her in action, not the way he had seen Zirkander blowing enemies up in his flier. It was probably silly, but she wanted to impress him.

"We can't see half of the walls from here," Kaika said. "Want to take a walk with me, Sire?"

She wanted to look at the bodies, too, to see if anything about the men's deaths could hint to the identity of their attackers, but first, they needed to make sure they were alone and see if there were, indeed, unauthorized back doors.

"Any time you like, Captain." Angulus smiled at her. It was a tired smile, or maybe one weary from responsibility.

Kaika decided it wasn't flirtatious—he certainly wasn't going to wink at *her*—but she liked it, nonetheless. He seemed human and approachable when his stern mask faded.

"Though a park or a beach would be a preferable place for it," he said with a sigh, and nodded for her to start on her investigation.

"Parks and beaches are boring, Sire. Unless pirates are involved."

Angulus walked alertly beside her, his rifle cradled in his arms and pointing toward the shadows. That pleased her.

"Do you run into many pirates at parks?" he asked.

"Once. But usually it's just ten-year-olds with swords playing at being pirates. That's why parks are boring." Kaika peered into the labs as they passed them.

"Go through that tunnel over there, Zirkander," Angulus said, "and check the sleeping quarters upstairs. There's also a generator down the stairs at the end that powers the lights and the instruments in the labs. See if anyone's hiding back there, or if there are any clues as to what happened."

"Yes, Sire."

Kaika and Angulus returned to the search in the chamber, pausing to open lab doors and look at the walls inside. The equipment-filled rooms were set up closer to the outside of the mountain than the chamber, so she doubted tunnels would have been bored in from that direction—they would have seen entrances on their way in. Still, she looked and listened for anyone who might be hiding under counters. She encountered a number of strange chemical scents and contraptions that reminded her of the Cofah volcano lab, though the Cofah hadn't possessed electricity, at least not out at that remote location. Iskandia always seemed to have a bit of an edge over the empire when it came to technology, but their numbers were small when compared to the empire's population and all of the land and resources it claimed. Keeping the juggernaut from rolling over them again always seemed a battle against the inevitable. Kaika hoped something here could change the tides.

A rumble sounded from deeper inside the mountain, and the vibrations of the floor increased. Dust trickled down from somewhere in the distance. Kaika rested a hand against a doorjamb, wondering if this was an earthquake and if the shaking would increase. Angulus had promised the glass walls of the labs were thick, but could thick glass still crack and break? She thought about stepping away from them, but the shaking did not intensify. She had experienced an earthquake on one of the volcanic islands in Cofahre's southern chain, but she couldn't remember ever feeling one in Iskandia.

"Is this normal?" Zirkander yelled down from the tunnel he had gone into.

Kaika winced at the loudness of his words. She couldn't help but feel they should be discreet and quiet in here.

"Not as far as I've heard in the reports," Angulus called back.

Kaika's walk along the wall of labs had taken her past the cylindrical construct in the middle of the chamber, and she glimpsed a dark hole in the cement wall behind it, a hole that hadn't been visible from the entrance. As soon as the trembling quieted, she strode toward it.

She crouched and peered into what turned out to be a low tunnel shaft no more than three feet high and wide. Her first thought was that it was a lava tube, as the rounded stone walls were smooth, and she had never seen a manmade cutting tool that could leave such tidily carved rock. There wasn't any rubble visible, and she couldn't tell if the tunnel had been there for eons or for days. It disappeared into darkness where it might have gone on for fifty feet or fifty miles. No, probably not miles. She wrinkled her nose at a faint scent that drifted to her on a draft. Bat guano and ancient mustiness.

"That's not normal, either," Angulus said from behind her, his voice grim.

"New since you were here last?"

"Yes. This must be what Colonel Troskar was referring to."

"It must connect with a passage or cave that has a link to the outside. I smell bats. Technically, I smell what bats leave around under them in their dens, but it amounts to the same thing."

"I imagine so."

Kaika touched a hand to one of the smooth walls and found it still slightly warm. Interesting. She didn't think rock drilled with a boring device would remain hot hours afterward. This warmth seemed to come from within, and she thought again of lava tubes, the way the slow creep of magma might heat the rock around it to the melting point. But if lava had done this, where was it? Not only was there no rubble in the tunnel, but the floor around the entrance remained clean. She doubted the scientists had run over to wipe up magma oozing all over the place.

"Walls are warm," she said, then rubbed the stone with her fingers.

She didn't feel any residue, and she highly doubted a bomb could have been responsible for forming a tunnel like this, but since she'd been brought out here as the demolitions expert, she figured there was a reason. Someone suspected explosives had been involved *somewhere*.

She did not smell anything on her fingers. Granted, one of Major Bruntingdor's bomb-sniffing dogs would have been better for the task, but she could usually smell the *residue* after the explosion, gunpowder or charcoal or the sour, salty scent of potassium nitrate, depending on the bomb's makeup.

"Shall we investigate?" Kaika asked, curious as to what lay at the other end. Were there spies hiding back there? Or had they already made an escape? Was it possible they had been the same people who had been piloting those fliers? Maybe the king's team had chanced across them when the spies had been fleeing for the shoreline. But if so, why had a sorceress been down on the ground? And why had the fliers attacked if they were busy fleeing, especially when they were invisible?

"Eventually, yes," Angulus said. "But we better wait for our backup."

Kaika glanced at him and caught an intrigued expression on his face. He crouched behind her, scrutinizing the tunnel.

She grinned. "You want to check it out yourself, don't you?"

"Yes, but I've already got people questioning my sanity tonight, and after losing the others, I'm..." He met her eyes and trailed off, maybe remembering that she was a lowly captain and not a confidante.

Too bad. She wouldn't have minded being a confidante. Not that she cared that much about the inner workings of the monarchy and the politics of the land, but he seemed like he could use someone to listen. She owed him a lot for the career she loved that he'd allowed her to have all those years ago, so she would gladly do so for him.

"Being impulsive doesn't make you insane," she said.

"Impulsive, yes. I suppose that's some of what's guided me tonight. I never used to be impulsive; I've always carefully measured my actions and thought of the consequences ahead of time."

How tedious. Kaika kept the opinion to herself.

"But lately..." Angulus leaned back on his heels, looking toward the tunnel he'd sent Zirkander to explore.

Checking to see if they were alone? Kaika perked up, intrigued that he might tell her something that he wouldn't want the general to hear.

"I shouldn't have lost my temper out there with them." Angulus waved toward the main entrance, toward the direction of the exterior ledge. "I've just been furious with myself over the kidnapping, over the fact that I needed rescuing." His mouth twisted downward in something between a frown and a sneer. "I never thought of myself as someone who was helpless, as someone who *needed* to be surrounded by bodyguards. The ease with which I was removed from office is disconcerting. A blow to the ego."

Kaika could understand that. She'd hated having to be rescued by Nowon during a mission in the eastern province. Like he'd said, it was a blow to the ego to need someone else as a babysitter. And Angulus hadn't even been doing something impulsive and risky when he'd been kidnapped. He'd probably been going about his average day, and then woken up in the back of that lighthouse, tied up and helpless to escape.

"So having my officers plotting against me out there, even if it was for my own good..." There was that grimace again.

"From what I heard, Zirkander didn't want anything to do with it."

"No, he's like you. Brash and impulsive and perfectly willing to go along with me on foolish missions."

Even though he smiled slightly, Kaika didn't know what to make of the statement. It didn't sound like a compliment, yet he looked pleased.

"It sounds like this mission is important, not foolish," she hazarded.

"It is, but kings aren't supposed to put themselves into positions where they might be killed, thus leaving the country in chaos over a succession that isn't firmly established."

"What positions *are* kings supposed to put themselves in?"

"Padded rooms without windows or pointy objects, if my staff had its druthers."

"No pointy objects at all?" Kaika quirked an eyebrow. "Doesn't sound like much fun."

"It's often not." He frowned at her slightly, perhaps wondering if that had been an innuendo.

She smiled innocently.

Footsteps sounded on the other side of the chamber, Zirkander heading over to join them.

"Nobody upstairs, Sire," he said. "Just some drawers and lockers left open, belongings hastily packed. Other rooms look like they were abandoned without even that much effort. Generator room's locked, and I haven't seen a key. Do you—oh, hells." He'd come close enough to see the tunnel. "I guess that answers the question as to whether or not that sorceress has been here."

"Oh?" Angulus asked. "Do sorceresses burn holes through mountains?"

Kaika touched the smooth rock again. She couldn't come up with another explanation, so she supposed magic was as good of a guess as anything.

"Well, their swords can. I saw Jaxi do something like that to get us into a pyramid." Zirkander crouched to peer into the dark passage. "Nothing so long though. That must have taken a lot of time and used a great deal of power. How far does it go back?"

"We were debating whether to check," Kaika said. "I think we should brashly and impulsively do so." She wriggled her eyebrows at Angulus. She didn't truly want to encourage him to risk himself, but if there were enemy spies roaming through caves back there, she wanted to find them, especially if they had killed those scientists. They also might have gathered information and made schematics of whatever prototypes were in here.

Zirkander's eyebrows arched. "I prefer being brash and impulsive from my cockpit, where I have two machine guns to back me up. And a lot of space to maneuver out of trouble."

"You're not as fun as I thought you were, sir," Kaika said. "I hope that doesn't disappoint Sardelle in the bedroom."

His already elevated eyebrows climbed further, and he looked toward Angulus. "Have you ever noticed that she says whatever's on her mind, no matter what your rank is in relation to hers?"

"Yes. I've decided to find it charming." Angulus's eyes narrowed. "I'm still debating whether I classify it that way when you do the same thing."

"That's all right. I'd be concerned if my king found me charming." Zirkander rose. "I'm thinking that I could fly around out there and look for matching exit holes. There might be some sign that whoever made this already left. There's no point in crawling around in tunnels if nothing's back there to find. I could also fly over the trees down there, see if our scientists are hiding outside for some reason. Unless we think they went in there." He pointed to the tunnel.

"I doubt it," Kaika said. "We saw that scrap of cloth stuck under the outer door. More likely something came out of here and scared them into running."

"I wondered if there might have been a smoke bomb or something else deadly that they ran from," Angulus said, "but the fans aren't on." He waved toward the high walls. Here and there, square grates lay flush with the stone, and there had been some in the labs too. "They shouldn't have simply run from whatever enemy breached this facility," he went on. "There were experienced soldiers stationed here to guard the scientists and their work."

"Sorcerers are a special kind of enemy." Zirkander shuddered.

Kaika remembered the fireball smashing into the other flier. She would never forget that.

"True, but they swore an oath," Angulus said. "I hope they're alive, but they were supposed to defend this facility with their lives if necessary. They knew the risks and volunteered for the job." He pointed in the direction of the two bodies that they had found. "I haven't looked yet. How were they killed?"

"One was garroted, and the other's throat was cut."

"Garroted?" Kaika frowned. "There's a Cofah operative who's known for doing that. I'll take a look."

Zirkander and Angulus spoke quietly as she jogged over and examined the bodies. She agreed with the general's assessment. One had died by knife, one by garrote—a real one, she guessed by the clean line, not an improvised one. Both men had been taken down from behind.

"Might be Seeker," she said when the others joined her. "Could be someone else who wanders around with a garrote, but if he's the one responsible, he works directly for the emperor."

"That's comforting," Zirkander said. "We wouldn't want garden-variety operatives harassing us."

"Seeker is good on rooftops and stealthier than a cat, but not the best when he doesn't catch his prey by surprise. Quick, but he's short and doesn't have much power. Plus, he never watches out for his feet, so sweep him if you end up in a fight."

"You've fought him often?" Angulus asked.

"Once. And then there were some... other kinds of meetings."

Zirkander didn't smirk at her, not exactly, but the glint in his eyes said he knew exactly what she was talking about. She shouldn't have been so open with him about her past.

"For obtaining information," she emphasized. "Before he knew I was Iskandian."

Angulus tilted his head. "You have an Iskandian accent."

"Not always. And I have other attributes that are globally appreciated." On that note, it was definitely time to change the subject. "Should we—"

Another rumble coursed through the floor. In the hallway, the hanging lights swayed on their chains. Kaika waited for the quake to subside and tried to determine if that had been stronger than the last one. Furniture wasn't falling in the labs, and a control panel on the giant cylinder glowed green without interruption. She thought about asking what that big construct was, but didn't want to pry into secrets the king didn't want her to know.

"Maybe the scientists left because of the earthquakes," Zirkander said.

"This area isn't known for its earthquakes," Angulus said.

"All the more reason to find their sudden appearance alarming. Maybe you should wait outside until Sardelle gets here, Sire."

"I want to look inside the labs first. I haven't figured out if anything was stolen yet. I can't imagine why these people would have broken in and killed people if they didn't want something."

"They could be scouts, just looking for information," Kaika said.

"Scouts aren't supposed to murder people and be noticed."

"That's generally true."

"If we leave, the spies could come back and have free rein of this place." Angulus nodded toward the small tunnel in the back. "That's unacceptable."

"So is getting flattened by falling rocks," Zirkander said.

"Nothing's fallen yet. But in case it does, you can be the heroic pilot that digs us out." Angulus flicked his fingers toward the exit. "Go do that recon you mentioned. See if you can find that hole and our people. Report back within two hours."

"Yes, Sire." Zirkander saluted, but paused to look at Kaika before leaving. "For your information, I'm *extremely* fun in the bedroom." He gave her a salute, too, a lazy two-fingered one, then headed for the exit. Over his shoulder, he added, "And also in caves, libraries, tents, theaters, pubs, and once in the cockpit of my flier, though I do not recommend that for reasons of comfort. Or rather discomfort."

Angulus frowned as Zirkander headed back toward the entrance. "I do *not* find that man charming."

Kaika wiped a grin off her face when he looked back at her.

"I don't, either, Sire. Pubs? People *eat* there. That's disgusting." Even as she finished speaking, she wondered if Angulus would be horrified by *her* list. She decided not to share it with him.

CHAPTER 6

NGULUS FLIPPED THROUGH NOTES IN a logbook. He had already searched the drawers and cabinets in all of the labs. Out in the main chamber, Kaika leaned against one of the glass walls where she could see the main tunnel and the new one. It had been over an hour since Zirkander left, and Angulus had not found a single enlightening thing. He rubbed his eyes, the late night catching up with him. A couple more hours, and it would be dawn. He supposed he shouldn't be frustrated that nothing was happening, other than the occasional shakes. That was for the best. Things could happen once he had a squad of well-armed soldiers in here, and Sardelle too.

A part of him wanted to invite Kaika in to chat with him and keep him awake—and maybe tell him stories of her adventures in Cofahre. He had a feeling that not *all* of the details had been included in her reports. But she was doing her job, staying alert and keeping watch, as a good soldier should. He shouldn't be a bad influence. He definitely shouldn't call her in and try to make witty conversation in an attempt to show her that he was *much* more interesting than Zirkander. Even if he hadn't had sex in a theater. Or a pub. Or, gods help him, a flier cockpit. Angulus was going to make sure to bring soap and a damp cloth the next time he climbed into any aircraft that Zirkander was piloting.

It wasn't that he was repressed... exactly. It was more that there were few places he could go without an audience of bodyguards, and he definitely wasn't an exhibitionist.

Another tremor shook the floor, made the lights sway, and rattled bottles on shelves, but it was no fiercer than any of the others, and he didn't bother setting down the binder in his hands. Until a cry rang out.

Though it sounded distant, the inhuman wail seemed to come

from all directions, even from within his own head. The power of it reverberated through him, and he found himself dropping the binder and grasping at the closest counter for support. The wail came again, completely alien, but at the same time, perfectly understandable. Whatever was uttering it was in pain.

A touch alighted on his arm. "Sire? Are you all right?"

Kaika stood next to him, her face calm but concerned. At first, he worried that she hadn't heard the noise, and that he was under some kind of isolated attack, but it sounded again, and she winced. Still, she kept hold of his arm, offering him support if he needed it.

Angulus straightened and nodded at her. He appreciated her solicitude, but he did *not* need support. The scream was affecting him strangely, but he could handle it.

"Yes," he said. "Can you tell where it's coming from?"

"I can't even tell what it is." Kaika looked through the window wall, toward the dark tunnel. "Some animal?"

"More than that, I think." Angulus touched his temple, trying to distinguish what he was hearing from what he was feeling inside of his skull. Maybe the latter was his imagination, an effect of the strange noise.

"Should we—"

Before Kaika could finish, the floor shook. Not the insignificant tremors of before, but fierce rocking motions that made Angulus think of being on a ship during a storm. He was thrown against the desk and grunted as his groin slammed into the edge. Something fell to the floor and shattered. The lamps flickered.

"We need to get out of here." Kaika grabbed his arm and stepped toward the door.

A filing cabinet toppled over inches from her face. Angulus pulled her back. More furniture was falling, with books and binders being hurled from shelves. One of the glass doors flew open, slamming against the wall with a crack. The thick glass did not shatter, but Angulus did not want to be running past it when it did.

"Over here," he barked as the lights flickered again. Once

more, the alien keening erupted from a distance, bouncing off the walls—and the insides of his skull.

Kaika let him tug her into the corner. Angulus ducked under a counter with room enough for two under it and pulled her down with him. It appeared sturdy, though he had no delusions about it holding up if the ceiling came down. But the facility had been designed to withstand bombs flung at it from outside. It should hold up to an earthquake—or whatever this was.

Kaika hesitated before crawling fully under the counter with him, but a lamp slamming to the floor convinced her to dive into the cubby. Angulus suffered an elbow to the ribs, but he wrapped his arms around her and pulled her close, not wanting her head sticking out, not when things were flying from the walls like bats scared out of a cave.

As the floor continued to heave, the wood supports of the counter groaned behind him. A thunderous crack came from the glass wall, followed by shards tinkling to the floor. He poked his head out from underneath the counter to eye the cement ceiling warily, worried the next crack would come from above.

The roar of noise that came next was from out in the testing chamber or in one of the tunnels leading from it. Cracks and snaps sounded, followed by heavy slabs crashing to the ground. Rockfall.

The lights flickered a final time and went out.

Angulus yanked his head back under the desk and closed his eyes. He pulled Kaika more tightly to him and wondered if this was the end for both of them. Should he have followed her and tried to make it out? Had he condemned them to a lonely burial within this mountain? Should he do something idiotic like kiss her before they were crushed?

Before he'd come to a decision on that last thought, the shaking quieted. Rocks continued to fall, but fewer in number and less frequent, each individual thump audible instead of the cacophony from seconds before. Soon the thumps dwindled, and the distant clatters grew infrequent. Angulus could hear his and Kaika's breaths. They were both breathing too quickly, too shallowly, terror setting the pace. He forced himself to deepen his breaths and tried to calm his body. In the darkness, he couldn't see anything and didn't know whether the ceiling inside their lab remained intact or not. He had no idea if they could find a way out. All he knew for certain was that Kaika was mashed against him, her shoulder pressing into his chest and her butt in his lap.

A bead of sweat dribbled down the side of his face, and dust coated his tongue. In the past, when he had imagined cuddling with Kaika, this wasn't how it had gone.

She stirred and started to say something, but her first word broke into a series of coughs. He found the back of her head and rested his hand in her hair. He wasn't sure what that was supposed to do, but his arm was pinned into the corner, and it was all he could manage. She had lost her cap. A silly thing to notice. Dust and tiny shards of cement and wood coated her hair, but it felt thick and soft beneath the debris. He resisted the urge to brush it clean. That was too familiar. Just because she was sitting in his lap and they were courting death didn't mean that he should be overly familiar. Probably. He wondered if he should have kissed her earlier. Now it would seem strange. Unless he was honest with her and told her that he'd had feelings for her for a long time. Here in the dark might be a good time. If she was horrified by the admission, he wouldn't be able to see it in her eyes.

She finished coughing and lifted an arm to wipe her face, clipping him in the nose with her elbow.

"Sorry, Sire," she said.

"No, *I'm* sorry," Angulus said, his throat scratchy. "Earlier today, or yesterday, I suppose it was, I considered asking you out for a fancy dinner, but I thought you'd find a dinner date too sedate to be interesting. Then I was made aware of the need for this excursion, and that we required someone with demolitions experience. It seemed a more natural way for us to, er. Well, I thought you might enjoy the mission." He paused, not wanting her to think the only reason he'd brought her along was because he wanted to get in her pants. Was it too late? Had that already been implied? If he rescinded it, would he make it worse? Better to press on. "So if we die here, you can blame it on me being too cowardly to ask you to dinner."

He hadn't wanted to see the rejection on her face, but as the silence dragged on without a response, he started to curse the darkness. She hadn't moved; she barely seemed to be breathing. What was she thinking?

"I'm a simple girl, Sire. You don't have to schmooze me with fancy food—or a fancy mission. All you have to say is, 'My place, tonight?' and I'll give you a yes or no without a lot of thought."

Her bluntness wasn't surprising, but it left him speechless for a moment. That *My place, tonight?* comment. Did she think he was only interested in sex? He supposed that was logical of her to assume—it wasn't as if kings courted and married commoners all that often—but the idea stung. Maybe because it implied she would only be interested in sex too. *If* she was interested at all. He hadn't missed that her statement hadn't answered the question she had proposed. Should he ask? He chickened out and said, "I'm less simple."

"No kidding."

Angulus laughed, then wished he hadn't because some of the dust in the air made its way down his throat, and he ended up coughing. He turned his head out of a notion that he shouldn't cough all over a woman he was discussing a relationship with. She didn't say anything while he wiped his eyes and recovered, trying to find his voice again. At least she didn't pull away from him. Not that there were many places to go. Something had fallen right beside his boot, and escaping the counter might prove difficult.

"*I'm* actually fairly simple," Angulus amended, "but the position can make my life complicated."

"Yeah."

"Kaika," he said slowly, not sure if he should make his other confession. Her responses hadn't been that encouraging thus far. "When you asked if you were being punished because of your new assignment... that was the furthest thing from my mind. You're right that others could train the young pilots, but I wanted to—and I know this is selfish—I wanted to keep you here in the city. Because in the past, I couldn't—I mean, when Nia was alive, I felt compelled to be faithful, or at least discreet with, uhm, brief indiscretions." Hells, what was he saying? Nothing cogent, that was certain. "What I mean is that I'd never wanted to be the kind of promiscuous philanderer that my father was. Don't get me wrong. He was a competent ruler, and I adored him as a boy, but his exploits with women were a joke around the castle. I know they hurt my mother, who loved him a great deal. So my point is—" Yeah, what was that point again? "—even though my second wife and I had an arranged marriage and were never in love with each other and I've, ah, admired you for a long time, I never felt that I could act upon that. Not to presume that you would have wanted to be acted upon." Seven gods, he didn't even know what that *meant*. He needed to blurt out his confession without any more of this tongue-tangling explanation. "Now that Nia is gone, I thought that if you were in the city for a while, I might find a chance to get to know you through more than reports."

There. He should have said that from the beginning. If she was used to men who spoke their minds comfortably, as he imagined most soldiers did, then she'd probably be repelled by his fumbled babbling.

The long silence that followed did not encourage him.

"You've read my reports?" she finally asked.

Her tone was difficult to read. She didn't sound horrified, but she didn't sound joyously enthused by his admission, either. She must think the entire situation bizarre and maybe surreal. Maybe he should have simply asked her to dinner, after all. At least then she wouldn't have been caught by surprise; surely, she knew what it meant when men asked her out for a meal.

"All of them," he said.

"I should have tried harder to make them legible."

Judging by the way she was pointedly not commenting on his confession, she must not want to deal with it. Maybe she wanted to pretend it hadn't happened. That hurt, but he wanted to give her a way out, if that was what she wanted.

"I've studied cryptography and multiple languages," he said.

"I was usually able to decipher them."

"That's good."

"Yes."

And with that, he had no idea what else to say. The trickle of debris falling out in the chamber had stopped, so maybe it was best to see if they could escape the confines of the counter. For more reasons than one. At least he'd proclaimed his interest. She could decide if that meant anything to her. Or not.

"Shall we see if we can get out of here?" Angulus lowered his arms as much as he could, so she wouldn't feel that he was holding her to him.

"Probably a good idea. But... Sire?"

He almost told her to call him Angulus, but he didn't. If she wanted to be something besides king and officer, then they could do that, at least in private. But for now, they needed to be professionals. "Yes?"

"Most of my gear is out on the ledge. I left the heavy stuff by the general's flier because I didn't know what we were going into or if we'd be attacked and need to be able to move quickly. I have a few things in my utility belt, but most of my explosives are out there. I can't blow us out if I need to." She sounded anguished, like she'd made a decision that would cost them their lives.

He found the idea of setting off explosives from *inside* of a mountain insane, but all he said was, "If it makes you feel better, I have no idea where my rifle is."

"Not really. You're not a soldier. It's not your job to stay snuggled up to your weapons around the clock."

Kaika sighed and wriggled out of his lap, clunking something—her head?—on the counter above them. That didn't keep her from continuing. Judging by the clatter and crunches, she was able to leave their corner and venture into the lab. He found that heartening. Maybe the rockfall would be off to the side and not hinder them.

"I also don't know where my lantern is," he said, shifting to hands and knees to crawl out.

"I have one in my gear. On the ledge." Another clatter announced her progress toward the door.

Angulus climbed to his feet and tried to follow her. He tripped over fallen furniture before he had gone more than two steps. Small mountains of wood and boxes and broken equipment cluttered his path. He ended up crawling to the door, only to cut his hand on broken glass.

"I'm out in the chamber," Kaika said.

"Is it as dark out there as it is in here?"

"Unfortunately, yes. Also..."

He groped his way to the door. "What?"

A rock shifted and fell. In the dark, Angulus struggled to get his bearings. It took him a moment to visualize the layout and discern where Kaika's voice—and that falling rock—had come from. A few more rocks scraped, then thudded to the floor. Kaika grunted. Was she trying to climb over something?

With the dread of certainty settling in his stomach, he said, "The entrance is blocked, isn't it?"

A few more rocks clunked, then it grew silent.

"Yeah," Kaika said, chagrin in her voice.

So much for his state-of-the-art facility being built to withstand bombings. The *chamber* had survived—as he padded toward Kaika's voice, he didn't run into any debris piles—but the engineers who had hollowed the place out apparently hadn't thought entrance tunnels were important.

He brushed against the cylindrical casing in the center of the chamber. The reminder of its presence, along with the big rocket housed within, spurred bleak thoughts. He might have been thinking sarcastically about the engineers, but the fact that the casing hadn't toppled over was reassuring. The last report he'd received had spoken of preparations for testing out in the eastern desert, so it was possible that this rocket was loaded with a deadly payload and ready to launch.

Angulus reached Kaika at the same time as a match flared to life.

"I found your lantern," she said.

"Good. I think."

The weak light did little to illuminate the cavernous space, but he could see what he'd already assumed, that the entrance tunnel was blocked and that the chamber itself had held up much better than the labs. Even in the labs, the structural damage was minimal; it was mostly the furnishings and equipment that had made a mess and left them cowering under a counter.

Angulus spotted his rifle lying on the floor amid shattered glass near the lab and remembered he had left it propped by the door. He was fortunate he hadn't needed to use it. He walked over and grabbed it before returning to the rubble-filled passage.

The cement ceiling of the tunnel had come down, along with countless tons of rocks above it. He couldn't tell if it was plugged all the way to the entrance or only for a few meters. If the latter, they *might* be able to dig their way out. He eyed some of the larger pieces, gauging their weight. With the supplies in the facility, they should be able to rig some pulleys to help.

"Do we try to dig out?" Kaika asked. "Or see if that other tunnel is in better shape? Because I don't want to be in here if the earth shakes again."

"Neither do I." Angulus stroked his chin, the thickening beard stubble scraping his fingers and attesting to how long of a day it had been. "But I would like to know *why* the earth is shaking."

The pained keening had stopped, at least for the moment. He wondered if it had been some harbinger of the earthquake. He seemed to remember a random piece of trivia that dogs knew earthquakes were coming before people felt them. Of course, whatever had made that noise hadn't been any dog.

"Volcanic activity?"

"It's been forty years since a volcano erupted in the Ice Blades, and you would have to go back hundreds of years to find mention of a significant earthquake in this part of the world." He headed toward the unauthorized tunnel as he spoke. They would *have* to explore it now. Just because the chamber had survived the last quake intact did not mean that another wouldn't bring down the ceiling—or damage the rocket and cause the explosives inside to blow this mountain to pieces. "I suspect this is a local phenomenon."

"I'll go first, Sire." Kaika jogged ahead of him as soon as she saw where he was going. "I may not have all of my gear with me, but I have enough." She patted the bulging pouches on her belt.

His first instinct was to object to letting a woman go first, but he reminded himself that Kaika was the experienced soldier here and probably more likely to survive danger than he. His ego did not want to accept that, but his rational mind won the battle. He spread his hand, inviting her to enter ahead of him.

Angulus followed right behind, half crouching and half crawling on his knees since the passage was less than half his height. Carrying the lantern and his rifle made the journey all the more awkward, but Kaika did not complain, and she was nearly as tall as he. She scrambled through the tunnel as easily as she had vaulted through that obstacle course on the training grounds. He sighed to himself, annoyed that he wasn't as agile, but he had broader shoulders and a thicker build. *That*, he told himself, was the only reason he was slower.

Kaika paused and looked back at him. They had gone about thirty meters, with the tunnel making a turn so that the chamber had already disappeared behind him. Not that he would have been able to see it, anyway—the lights had not come back on.

"You don't have to wait for me," Angulus said. "I'll catch up."

"I'm sure you will, but I thought you might have insight into this hole." She pointed at something on the ground in front of her.

Not a something, he realized as he drew closer. A *lack* of something. The tunnel continued on ahead, the same uniform three feet in diameter, but a similar-sized hole opened up in the ground. Kaika knelt at the edge, peering downward. A thick cable came out of the hole and disappeared into the dark passage ahead of them.

"My insight has been lacking in all regards tonight," Angulus said, squeezing in beside her, his shoulder bumping against her back. "Sorry."

He doubted she would object to touching, given the circumstances, but he *had* just been telling her about his dinner date fantasies. If he had made her uncomfortable, she might find this forced closeness awkward.

"Sorry for bumping me or sorry for lacking insight?" She

looked at him, her face only a few inches from his, her lean features warmed by the soft lantern light. Angulus had meant to look into the hole, but he found himself gazing into her eyes, noticing that they were more hazel than brown and appeared almost green in this light. They had never been this close before, and even though it should have been the last thing on his mind, he thought about kissing her. She had full, inviting lips. At least they seemed inviting to him, though she wasn't offering one of those sultry smiles she was very good at. She was probably waiting for him to answer her question.

He pulled his gaze from her lips and opened his mouth. Er, what had her question *been*?

"Yes," he said. "All of that. Uhm, let me take a peek."

"All right." One of her eyebrows arched. "At the hole, right?"

"Yes." What else would he have looked at?

This time, her lips did curve up into a smile, and he had a feeling he had missed a chance to say something playful or witty. Or both. Damn it.

He lowered the lantern into the hole and leaned forward as far as he could. To his disappointment, she shifted to the side to give him more room. Touching had been nice.

Focus, he growled at himself and dipped his head below the edge.

"Huh," he murmured. "It doesn't go straight down. It angles back and looks like it goes under us, toward the way we just came." He leaned his head down further, twisting to lower the lantern.

Kaika dropped a hand to the back of his belt, as if she could hold him back if he was foolish enough to lean out too far and fall in. He would probably end up taking both of them into the hole where they would tumble down to the bottom. The slope would be climbable, but it was steep.

"It's a good sign when a woman grabs your belt, right?" Angulus prodded the cable and suddenly realized what it was.

"More so when she grabs the buckle than the back of your belt."

"Ah, that's unfortunate. You were getting my hopes up."

"I *am* checking out your ass, if that helps."

Angulus pulled up so quickly, he conked his head on the low ceiling. He barely noticed. "Really?" His voice sounded alarmingly squeaky in his ears. A man at his age really should be better at flirting.

She didn't answer his question. Her eyes were twinkling, but Angulus couldn't tell if she was amused because they were flirting and she was liking it, or if she was just amused by his ineptness at the game.

"Anything interesting in the hole?" she asked.

He thought about pretending to misunderstand which hole she was talking about, but didn't want to risk being crude. Besides, they had more important things to worry about. Even though this tunnel had survived the last quake, he would prefer not to be trapped in it when another came.

"I think it goes to the generator room I mentioned." Angulus pointed at the cable. "Someone is siphoning our electricity for something."

"Something? Like they want fancy lamps of their own?"

"I don't think you would go through all the effort of drilling a long tunnel and killing people for lamps." He waved for her to lead the way past the opening. "Let's continue on. Follow the cable."

"Is it possible they didn't *want* to kill people? That your two scientists got in the way? Caught them stealing the electricity?"

"I suppose it's possible," he said as he scrambled around the hole, banging his knee on the edge and clunking his head on the ceiling again. "But why would they have drilled into the main chamber then? Why not go directly to the generator?"

"Wrong turn?"

"Even if the first tunnel was an accident, they would have been discovered eventually by going to the generator room. It has to be filled with fuel every day."

"Maybe they found out there were secret research projects in the big cave, got greedy, and decided to try to get those too."

"Then why was everything still there?"

Kaika shrugged. "When we find them, I'll hold them down so

you can question them."

Angulus thought of his two dead men. "I'd like that very much."

The tunnel cut around a corner again, and Kaika slowed down. "Light ahead," she murmured. "Better turn down the lantern."

Maybe the electricity thieves *were* powering lamps. But surely, there must be more to it than that.

She kept going, a pistol in hand and her rifle across her back, just shy of scraping the edges of the walls. He clambered after her, doing his best not to make noise. Somehow, she was moving without making a sound, while he kept clunking his rifle—and himself—against the walls.

As they drew closer to the source of light, Angulus cut out the lantern. He bumped the cable with his toe and thought about cutting *that* too. If he dropped whoever was up there into darkness, maybe they could more easily attack their foes. But it would also warn them that something was wrong. They would be more prepared for someone coming out of the tunnel.

In the end, he did nothing. He continued after Kaika and tried not to feel superfluous.

After easing around a final corner, the tunnel straightened, and the exit came into view. He scooted closer to Kaika, so that he could see over her shoulder better, and also so he could protect her back, the same way she was determined to protect his.

All that lay visible beyond the tunnel was an open area, with a rock wall at the far end. At least one hundred meters across. Whatever they were about to enter, it was a cavernous space. A soft yellowish light illuminated it, but he couldn't guess at the source. It was far more powerful than a few lanterns or candles would be, and it had a different hue than the harsh lamps in the facility. The wall he could see in the distance appeared to be natural, suggesting a cavern rather than a space hollowed out by man. Angulus frowned at the idea that the engineers who had chosen this mountain for the building of his secret facility hadn't noticed that there were giant caves in the backyard. If they had, they might have anticipated someone burrowing in from back here.

Kaika paused a few feet from the mouth of the tunnel and tilted her ear toward the exit. Angulus hadn't heard voices or any indications that people waited for them, but he stopped to listen too. He thought he detected a faint regular ticking.

Kaika looked back at him, her eyes troubled. "Problem," she mouthed. "Possibly a *big* problem."

CHAPTER 7

MAYBE IT WAS A CLOCK. A nice big grandfather clock sitting in the middle of a hidden cavern, cheerily ticking away for the bats.

"Yeah, sure," Kaika muttered under her breath.

Judging by Angulus's expression, he hadn't figured out the implications yet. He didn't work with explosives for a living. Kaika thought about explaining, but in case time was limited, she had better not dawdle. Besides, there might be people out there, people who could overhear them. Of course, they would have to be suicidal people if her guess proved right.

Hoping she was wrong and that something innocuous was responsible for the sound, Kaika eased forward. A draft whispered across her cheeks, smelling of bat guano and ancient mustiness but of the outdoors, as well, moss and fir trees. Maybe she and Angulus would be able to escape without dealing with the problem she suspected awaited inside.

When she reached the opening, she had intended to glance in every direction, hunting for enemies, but she ended up gawking at the unexpected sight.

A huge limestone cavern stretched out in front of her, a dry streambed meandering between natural pillars that supported the towering ceiling. She barely noticed the terrain. Along one wall stood a row of enormous statues of crouching dragons, each one different in size and pose, though each had its wings folded about its body to fit into the cavern. Each was also perched on a pedestal, the talons of their big lower legs curled over the edges. The pedestals were placed at regular intervals, and she counted ten of the grayish statues. The statue at the end, barely visible from her vantage point, was only half gray with the top half a bright coppery gold. Wires had been draped all over the statues, linking each one in a chain, and even from a distance, she could see brown paper packages poised on the heads of the dragons. Explosives. She didn't have to be close enough to read the stenciling on the packages to know they were Cofah Army RSF-45s. The biggest, most powerful explosives their military used. She couldn't see the clock ticking down to detonation yet, but it had to be in there somewhere. The soft ticks echoed through the quiet cavern.

"What in all the cursed realms is this?" Angulus breathed, resting a hand on her shoulder as he leaned forward to peer out.

Another time, she would have contemplated how she felt about that hand on her shoulder, especially in lieu of his startling but intriguing revelations, but now, she barely registered it.

"No idea, Sire," Kaika whispered, tearing her gaze from the explosives to see if anyone else was in the chamber. She doubted she would find anyone—people didn't usually set timers for bombs and then loiter in the area—but she couldn't assume that.

Nobody was standing out in plain sight, but the copious pillars offered numerous hiding places. Glowing lamps that reminded her of flier power crystals had been mounted on the long wall opposite the dragons. They created deep shadows among the statues and behind stalagmites and pillars. Any of those shadows could hold a threat—an *additional* threat. It would take ten minutes to run through the entire place and check all of the nooks.

Angulus shifted behind her. "Let me out, please."

Kaika hesitated. Should she presume to tell him to stay put, to let her do a thorough check before releasing him? Did she have *time* to do a thorough check? Her body twitched, wanting to propel her toward the source of that ticking. They might have hours until the explosion, or they might have minutes.

"Can you stay here while I look around?" Kaika eased to the side and stood, her legs relieved after crouching for so long.

"I can, but I won't." Angulus stood beside her and hefted his rifle. "Go find the timer. I'll look for threats."

She hated to let him expose himself, but with only two of them, his orders made sense. "Yes, Sire."

Before either of them could go far, the keening wail they had heard before sounded, this time much more loudly. Kaika cupped her hands over her ears. It didn't help. The bizarre noise banged around in her skull like a clapper in a bell. She felt it— the pain of whatever creature was making it—with her entire body, and a strange power accompanied it, almost forcing her to her knees. The ground shuddered, and she stumbled backward, bracing herself against the rock wall.

Angulus gripped the wall beside her, a pained grimace crossing his face. Kaika worried the shaking would escalate, that they would have to suffer through another large quake, this time without a counter to hide under. But the tremors did not last long or increase in force. The wail faded away, and the shakes along with it. As the last of the tremors disappeared, Kaika stared up at the explosive atop the closest statue. Its perch on the dragon's head, resting between a horn and a ridge that thrust up from the skull like a bad hairdo, seemed tenuous.

"Need to do something about those," Kaika said.

Not waiting for a response, she jogged toward the statues, glancing left and right as she did so, knowing she was risking herself by running into the open. Nothing stirred. Not even a bat, though layers of guano coated the floor, and she crunched through a crust. Lots of other footprints had punctured that top layer too. She might have found useful information in those prints if she'd had more time to look, but she was too busy peering into the alcoves between the statues, looking for a ticking clock.

Why someone wanted to blow up a bunch of statues, she couldn't guess. She also couldn't guess what those statues were doing here in the first place.

Maybe Angulus had an idea. She glanced back, the question on her lips. He was frowning into the shadows behind a stalagmite. She would wait until later to ask. It was probably a question for an archaeologist to answer. All that mattered for now was nullifying the explosives, or, if that couldn't be done easily, finding an exit to the outside. But dealing with the bombs would be ideal. Given that the facility was full of weapons, some of them probably explosives, having bombs go off this close could be a very bad thing. The earthquakes were troubling enough. If the bombs in here went off, it could bring down the entire mountain. She had a flash of insight as to why those Cofah fliers—and the sorceress—might have been so far away from here. Maybe they had been the ones to leave these bombs, and they'd been escaping, making sure they got far enough away not to be hurt by the collapse. Maybe the fliers had even been coming to pick up the sorceress when the Iskandians chanced upon them.

As Kaika got closer to the end of the row of gray statues, she stumbled on uneven rock, blurting a curse as she got a better look at the multi-hued one. She stared, unable to parse what she saw before her, even forgetting the bombs for a moment.

The bottom half of the dragon appeared as the others, gray stone—or what she had first taken for stone—but the golden top half seemed alive. It *had* to be alive. It was bleeding. Two long lances had been thrust through the creature, one going through its shoulder, pinning the wing to its chest with the point sticking out on the back side, and the other cutting through the side of its neck. That one looked like a mortal wound, but drops of blood were dribbling from the puncture, leaving a streak down its scaled torso. Dead dragons didn't bleed, did they? The creature's eyes were closed, but its face, reminiscent of a cross between a lizard and a wolf, wore an expression that seemed the equivalent of a human grimacing in pain.

Wires stuck out of the ends of the lances and trailed down the dragon's wing and across the floor to a square box on the ground with a couple of switches sticking out of it. The air around the box and the dragon hummed, reminding Kaika of being caught out in an electrical storm. There was an odor, too—charred meat.

"Uhm, Sire?" Kaika glanced back, wondering if he'd seen this yet and what he made of it.

He was only a dozen steps away, holding his rifle and watching her back. She was supposed to be watching *his* back, but this wasn't the time to point that out.

"I have no idea," he said softly. "Have you found the timer?"

Kaika flinched. How could she have forgotten, even for a few seconds? The dragon was an oddity, but it didn't appear dangerous in its current condition. The explosives were another matter.

She ran toward the box on the floor. It didn't appear to have anything to do with the explosives, as its only wires were hooked to the ends of the lances, but maybe the clock was nearby. She almost tripped over a black cable, the same one they had been following through the tunnel. It connected to the back of the box. They had found the receptacle for their stolen electricity.

In the shadows of the wall next to the dragon, Kaika spotted the timer, a clock face attached to a detonator with all manner of wires running out of it. It looked like a mess, like someone hadn't known exactly what he had been doing. That could make it more dangerous than explosives laid by a professional.

"Wonderful," she muttered, racing toward it.

A giant, dusty bronze plaque was mounted on the wall above the detonator. She could make out writing, something old and in a language she didn't recognize. There wasn't time to do more than register the plaque's presence. Whatever it said, she doubted it had anything to do with the explosives.

Angulus was on the move again, finishing his search of the chamber. She would be on her own for this.

Kaika dropped to her knees in front of the detonator, careful not to touch anything. She had dealt with Cofah bombs before and knew they tended to be less stable than their Iskandian counterparts. She'd seen a crate of them go up in a fiery explosion when men loading it onto a dirigible had lost their grip and dropped their load to the ground. That had been a gory mess. Each of the explosives she had passed had been balanced atop the heads of the frozen dragons. One inadvertent tug of a wire could start a chain reaction that would bury her and Angulus.

"Sire, there's only thirty minutes left on the timer," Kaika said.

"Can you disarm it?"

"I know how, but a lot of things can go wrong. I'd rather not try with you here. Or anywhere near this mountain." Thinking about what could have happened if they hadn't come to check out this chamber made her hands shake. They could have died in a fiery explosion that would destroy the mountain without a clue as to where it had come from or why. At least this way, there was a chance to survive. Thirty minutes wasn't a lot, but she could work with it. "What do you think about finding wherever that draft is coming from and going to flag down Zirkander?"

"You want me to leave you here? *Alone?*"

"Better one person than many if things don't go well." Kaika dug pliers, wire cutters, and tweezers out of her explosives kit. It was a good thing she always kept that gear on hand. "I could go find Zirkander with you, and we could let these statues get obliterated, but I'm assuming it would not be good if bombs went off in close proximity to your labs."

"You are correct. And as far as me leaving, if the rocket in the facility goes off, it won't matter if I get a thirty-minute head start."

Twenty-nine minutes now.

"Also," Angulus added, "I don't think these are statues."

Kaika glanced up at the bleeding dragon, but she wasn't ready to analyze what he was saying yet. She focused on the detonator and went back to work. "Let's get this disarmed then. I—"

A shot rang out, almost deafening in the enclosed cavern. At the same instant, something slammed into her lower back. Pain exploded, and she gasped, falling forward. She kept the presence of mind to catch herself with her hands, not letting any part of her body land on the detonator. Even with her training, it took her a long second to realize she had been shot.

Hearing another shot and a roar of fury snapped her out of her stunned state, and she pushed herself back up, yanking her pistol from its holder. She spotted two men in the shadows across the cavern, crouching behind a massive column. She recognized one, the Cofah garrote specialist, Seeker. A second man she didn't know stood at his side, a rifle in his hands. Seeker riveted her attention, because his pistol was pointed straight at her, smoke wafting from the barrel.

She saw her death in his eyes, knew he was about to fire again and knew also that she had nothing to hide behind. But then his gaze flickered to the side, toward the roaring person.

Angulus barreled into Seeker, taking him to the ground. Without hesitation, Kaika shot the second man. He had skittered back, avoiding Angulus, and wasn't focusing on her.

Her shot took him in the shoulder. She cursed her aim—her stupid fingers seemed numb with shock, and she almost dropped her pistol.

"Quit it," she snarled at her fingers. She'd been shot before. She wasn't going to fall apart and be unable to perform her duty here, not when Angulus was engaged in a fight he probably couldn't win and there was a second Cofah with a gun.

The shot man grabbed his shoulder and lunged toward the column. Aware of Angulus wrestling with Seeker, she willed her hand to steady. She fired a second shot an instant before her foe made it behind the rock formation. The bullet cracked into the side of his skull, and his head whipped sideways. He stumbled and collapsed at the base of the column.

Kaika tried to get to her feet, but pain blasted outward from her back. She fumbled and fell to her hands again. Hot warmth soaked her shirt, and the fabric rasped against the wound. Strange that she found that almost more annoying than the pain, but she couldn't do anything about either problem.

She lifted her head. She'd managed to keep the pistol, and she had more shots, but black dots swam through her vision. Trying to blink them away, she focused on Angulus. She couldn't shoot his enemy, not when they were wrestling on the ground. Seeker had gained the advantage, shifting to the top, and she raised her pistol. She had four more shots, plenty to kill the man, but her hand was shaking, and she didn't trust her aim. Before she could steady it, Angulus clobbered the Cofah agent in the chin, knocking him to th e side. He threw himself after Seeker, and they writhed about again, each trying to gain the top position.

Once more, Kaika tried to stand, but her legs were numb and wouldn't cooperate. Fine. She would crawl over there then. She wasn't going to let one little bullet keep her from doing her duty. Besides, she hadn't told Angulus that she found his story of wanting to get to know her flattering, and that she would love to have dinner with him. He better not get himself killed.

CHAPTER 8

HANDS WRAPPED AROUND ANGULUS'S NECK, hands much stronger than seemed possible. Somehow, the man had squirmed behind Angulus and had him from behind. He had the weight advantage and more muscle than his opponent, but the wiry Cofah agent was fast and harder to keep ahold of than a castle page caught in a lie. Angulus didn't usually appreciate his big build and the fact that he had a neck like an ox, but it served him well now. Even though the agent's fingers dug in, he gritted his teeth, flexing the muscles that protected his throat.

The man's weight shifted, and one hand loosened slightly. Angulus threw his elbow backward. Though the agent almost shifted out of the way, Angulus landed a glancing blow. Something fell on the ground, thin double wires attached to two wooden handles.

He barely registered the weapon, other than to realize this might be Kaika's garrote man—Seeker?—the one who didn't pay enough attention to his footwork. It would be hard to take advantage of that from the ground.

Angulus jabbed backward with another elbow and twisted around. He struck nothing but air. His opponent was scrambling to his feet and drawing a knife. Angulus jumped up, raising his fists, though they would not be much protection against a blade. He wished he had his rifle. Instead, alarmed at Kaika's injury, he'd shot wildly, missed, and charged in with bare hands. Some strategy.

Seeker lunged toward him, his hand moving so quickly it seemed to blur. The blade lashed toward Angulus's stomach. He scrambled to the side and threw out a wild block, hoping to hit the man's forearm instead of the sharp dagger. The blade nicked him, but he managed to turn it aside. He followed the block by leaping in and punching at the agent's face. Seeker jerked his head back, but could not completely evade the blow. Angulus caught him in the jaw. Instead of retracting his punch, he opened his fingers for a grab. But the agent had recovered and was trying to skitter away. Angulus caught his sleeve before he could put too much space between them. The blade slashed toward him again, the angle awkward now since Angulus was to the side. Remembering Kaika's advice, he kicked at the same time as he deflected the knife swipe.

His boot struck Seeker's shin. The man grunted, his gaze flicking downward for an instant. This time, Angulus succeeded in grabbing his foe by the scruff of the neck. He jumped to the rear and pulled the agent backward. Seeker attacked again with the knife, this time a wild stab as he toppled off balance. Angulus caught his wrist, turned it against the joint, and ripped the weapon out of his hand. With one hand still tangled in the agent's hair, he intended to jab the blade into his back, but the man twisted, bringing up a knee for a kick. Angulus thrust the knife at his chest.

He had never stabbed a man before, had only trained with practice blades in the gym, and he'd been warned about hitting ribs, but feeling the blade barely dig in and crunching against bone was another matter. In a surge of panic, he reversed his attack, certain the agent would recover. He slashed at his foe's throat as the man landed a kick to Angulus's knee. The blow sent pain lancing up Angulus's leg, and he stumbled backward, but it was too late to matter for the Cofah agent. Angulus's wild swing had been more effective than his opponent's calculated kick. The agent collapsed.

Angulus leaned back, his arms shaking. He needed a moment to catch his breath, but he couldn't take it. There had been a second Cofah, and there was—Kaika! Fresh panic clutched his heart at the memory of seeing her shot.

He whirled toward the detonator she had been working on, forgetting about the second enemy. He feared he would find her lying on the ground, unconscious—or worse. Instead, she knelt on one knee with her elbow propped on the other, her pistol held in both hands. It was pointing at the ground now, but he realized she must have been aiming toward his fight, waiting for a chance to fire.

"Guess you didn't need my help, Sire." She smiled, though it came across more as a grimace. Blood smeared one of her hands, and he had seen the bullet strike her. There was no chance it had missed.

Angulus wanted to sprint to her, but he paused to look for the second Cofah agent. Fortunately, the man lay unmoving beside the rock column, blood pooling underneath his head. His eyes were frozen open.

"No, but you look like you could use mine." Angulus ran across the chamber and dropped to his knees beside her.

"Do I? That's distressing." Kaika tried to put away her pistol, but missed the holster twice before snarling and jamming it in.

Angulus wanted to gather her in his arms and carry her to safety, but he had no idea where that might be. Even if they found an exit to the forest, they still wouldn't be safe. The clock had ticked down to twenty-five minutes. It seemed like his battle had lasted much longer than that. He gripped her shoulder and her arm, trying to support her without hurting her.

He leaned around to look at her back and spotted the bullet hole in her fatigue jacket. The dark material hid the blood, but he could tell it was damp. She didn't seem to be bleeding a lot, but he should fashion a makeshift bandage until... until what? He didn't know. One of the scientists working on the project had a medical background, but until they found that person, they had nothing. He'd had extremely basic first-aid training in the military, but that had been long ago, and he'd never had to put it to practical use.

"What do you want to do?" he asked, hating that he felt helpless. He was the king; he was supposed to know what must be done.

"Finish disarming the detonator," she said without hesitation. "Help me back, will you? My legs aren't working that well."

He hurried to obey, slipping his arms around her and carefully lifting her to her feet. "I should make a bandage for you."

"In twenty-four minutes, if we're still alive, you can do anything you want to me." She wriggled her eyebrows. Her face was pale, and her eyes crinkled with pain, but she managed a halfway convincing leer.

"Have you decided you *want* me to do things to you?" He would have wriggled his eyebrows back, but was too busy judging his question. He had meant it to be funny, to distract her from her pain, but he feared it had been crude. At the least, it wasn't articulate. Why couldn't he manage some of Zirkander's ease with her?

"You caught me by surprise back there, but I'm cozying up to the idea."

Angulus almost kissed her, but that would have been ludicrous timing. She was also cozying up to a bullet at the moment. He settled her on the ground in front of the detonator.

"Can I help with anything?" He eyed the tremor in her hands with concern.

"Just—"

An unearthly moan filled the chamber, making Angulus think of stories of undead monsters that supposedly haunted cemeteries on Spirit Walk Night. He looked up at the dragon beside them, its legs and lower body trapped in the stone-like material that comprised—or coated—the rest of the figures. The dragon was still bleeding, drops dripping down its scales, but now its eyes were open.

The eye closest to them swiveled downward to stare straight at Angulus. Even though the dragon was trapped and must be close to dead, it had an aura, a *presence*, that made him want to sink to his knees and plead for his life.

"Take care of that," Kaika finished.

"I think I'd rather work on the bombs."

"Too bad." She picked up the pliers that had fallen on the ground. "Soldiers deal with bombs. Kings deal with dragons. It's a rule."

Human. The voice sounded in his head, long and drawn out and filled with power. Power and pain.

Angulus backed away from Kaika, both so he wouldn't distract her and also so the dragon wouldn't pay attention to her. Its powerful lower legs and the bottom half of its wings were frozen in stone or whatever that was, but he wagered it could still do them harm. Angulus had seen Zirkander's reports of dealing with the other dragon, and he'd read enough history books to know that they were the source of all magic and that they could do much with nothing more than their minds.

Reminding himself that he was a king, not just some puny human, Angulus lifted his chin and stared the dragon in the eye. "What do you want, dragon?"

Free me.

Angulus considered the creature. His first instinct was to say no, or at least not right now, but what if it could help them? According to the history books, some dragons had been allies to humans long ago. Some had also been foes, aligning themselves with enemy nations. And others had preyed upon humans, the same way they preyed upon antelope and sheep. There was already one dragon that Angulus knew little about flying around in his country. He couldn't see adding another unknown element to the mix, especially one that would be extremely powerful when it healed from its injuries. This was a gold dragon, and the texts said they had been even stronger than the silver dragons such as the one Zirkander and the others had freed.

"In exchange for what?" he asked. It might not be wise to outright deny the dragon.

Kaika frowned over at him, but quickly returned her concentration to her work. She had snipped two wires and removed the clock from the rest of the device. He hoped that was going well. He also hoped her frown didn't mean that she didn't approve of his question.

The dragon's eyes closed partway, but the pupils, black slits in yellow irises, continued to bore into Angulus.

Free me, it said again, power lacing the words, making them a command.

Angulus caught himself taking a step toward the electrical box on the floor, but he stopped himself. Annoyance flared as he felt certain that the dragon was attempting to use some mind magic on him. He would not allow himself to appear subservient or contrite in front of this creature.

"I am King Angulus Masonwood the Third, thirty-seventh ruler of Iskandia. I will *not* be ordered around by some animal."

Animal! the dragon roared in his mind, making Angulus rethink his stance on contriteness. *Dragons made this world their home when your kind were beating your chests and howling at each other from the treetops.*

"Dragons have gone from this world. Humans rule here now."

Gone? The dragon's yellow eyes opened wide again.

Before Angulus could decide if he wanted to explain, a presence slammed into his mind. He gasped, staggering backward and reaching for his rifle. Something that felt like a rake scraped through his mind, scattering his thoughts like dried leaves. Was this an attack? He could barely think straight.

He'd no sooner than managed to find the trigger of his rifle than the presence disappeared from his mind. Having it withdraw was almost as much of a jolt as when it had first entered. He found himself leaning his hands on his knees, supporting himself. If the rifle hadn't been on a strap, he would have dropped it.

You know very little, the dragon commented. *Especially for a king.*

Angulus ignored the jab. He thought the creature sounded slightly less supercilious. Had it searched his mind and seen the truth there, that dragons were no more? Unless one counted the single creature that Zirkander's team had rescued. He grimaced, hoping this dragon hadn't found that thought, but it probably had. If it escaped, would it try to contact Phelistoth? And if so, what would come of that contact? Angulus wasn't certain he should think of Phelistoth as an ally yet, not when it had originally come from the Cofah Empire. Even if Phelistoth had been an Iskandian dragon, he wouldn't be sure how far to trust it. And what about this creature? What did it mean that it was here in this cave? Encased in stone? Was it a prisoner? Some Cofah-aligned dragon that Angulus's ancestors had figured out how to trap long ago? If so, it wouldn't think kindly upon the king of Iskandia.

He looked up, wondering if the dragon was reading his every thought.

The creature's eyes had closed, and its head hung. Its mouth never opened, but something akin to a groan escaped its throat—and its mind. The ground shivered in response. Angulus should have realized it right away, but only now did he see that those wails had originated from the dragon, and the earthquakes must have too. Some magic-powered side effect of its agony?

"Sire," Kaika whispered, her eyes tense and full of pain when she looked back at him.

That expression made his heart ache. Angulus wanted to run over and comfort her, not stand here and talk with a strange dragon.

"I think you should take the sticks out." She glanced up at the eight-foot lances skewering the dragon. Sticks. Hardly that.

"You're right. Its pain is putting us in danger."

Kaika frowned, disappointment flashing across her face. She opened her mouth, but closed it again, then nodded and went back to work. He had the distinct impression that she'd been thinking of putting a halt to the creature's misery, not protecting their own asses. Maybe he was being a heel for not seeing the dragon as a being in pain and wanting to alleviate that, but he worried about what it would do if it had its full power. Dealing with it now, even in pain, he had the sense that it could kill him. Maybe it *would* kill him if he didn't help it. But wouldn't it be better to keep it weak until he figured out if it was a threat to his nation?

Still, he found himself walking toward the box. Not because of anything the dragon was doing to him, but because of that expression from Kaika. He didn't want to disappoint her. Ever.

Maybe they would get lucky, and the dragon would be grateful to them for helping.

As he knelt to examine the box, he caught the dragon looking down at Kaika. He couldn't begin to interpret its facial expressions, but he hoped it had nothing inimical in mind.

"Dragon," Angulus said, to draw its attention back to him.

"Who did this to you?" He pointed toward the lances. "And why?"

It had to have been the Cofah operatives, but how had they known these statues were here? And why had they come only to blow them up?

Humans. The other humans.

No kidding. "Why?"

The box hummed softly. Angulus found a control panel under a hinged flap, but there weren't any instructions, and he wasn't sure if he should randomly flip switches and turn dials. He might end up electrocuting the dragon. Though that would solve one of his problems, he couldn't bring himself to contemplate killing a sentient creature that hadn't done any harm to him, at least not intentionally.

Instead of fiddling with the dials, he unscrewed the electrical cable from the back. It made his arm tingle painfully, and the box issued an annoyed *blizzzt*, but then the humming stopped.

The dragon inhaled sharply. Angulus backed away to see its face better. The head nearly brushed the cavern ceiling over thirty feet above them. This gold was the largest of the statues, and he wondered if it had been in charge of whatever this group of dragons had been.

"You want me to take the lances out?" Angulus thought the creature might bleed to death if he removed the one in its neck, but he knew nothing of dragon anatomy or a dragon's ability to heal itself.

Free me from my cage first, human king. The dragon's breaths were short and shallow. *Then I can use my magic to heal myself.*

"Cage?" Angulus eyed the lower half of the dragon, the half that still appeared to be carved from stone.

Kaika glanced back at him. Was she hearing the dragon's half of the conversation?

The crystal holds me, and I haven't the strength to destroy it. The dragon's eyes shifted to look straight across the cavern to what Angulus had taken for a lamp mounted on the opposite wall.

There was one in front of each statue. For the first time, he noticed that this dragon's crystal had been damaged. It still glowed, but its glow was weaker than the others, and broken pieces lay on the ground under it. From here, they appeared as transparent shards of glass.

Could these crystals truly have the power to encase dragons in stone without killing them? Angulus had read Zirkander's report and knew Phelistoth had supposedly been placed in stasis for thousands of years because of an illness. Had something similar been done here? He shivered at the idea that he might be unleashing some ancient deadly illness that could affect his people.

Destroy it, the dragon commanded. *The rest of the way. Then remove these stakes. I will heal, and then I will help you escape.*

Some of the creature's haughtiness had faded, and it sounded sincere. But did they *need* the dragon's help? Angulus had been smelling the earthiness of the forest since they entered this cavern, so he assumed there was a hole or cave mouth somewhere. If the Cofah sorceress had entered and then left after she and her people had done this to the dragon, the exit should be large enough for humans.

Perhaps he should find out if the dragon could heal Kaika. He knew Sardelle had that power. If the dragon had magic, magic that was supposedly greater than anything humans possessed, could it heal too?

The exit is not clear, the dragon told him.

Images appeared in his mind, of their cavern winding through the rocks for a quarter mile, then coming to an opening, one that had been drilled—or melted—through an ancient rockfall. Daylight seeped in through the passage, which appeared similar to the one Angulus and Kaika had already crawled through. He was about to say as much, but the dragon showed him another image: two men and a woman walking through the cavern to the passage. The woman wore golden armor and carried a sword, the hilt glowing a soft silver. The sorceress? Angulus had never seen her, but that armor matched what Zirkander had written up in his report about attacking the sky fortress. How long had she been back in Iskandia, and how had she found this place? Angulus recognized the men with her as the ones he and Kaika had fought and felt confused. If they had left, why did they return?

In the vision, the trio stopped in front of the tunnel, and one of the men held up a small package wrapped in brown. Another bomb, this one smaller than the ones perched on the statues. The woman spoke to them, gesturing back in the direction of the dragons. Angulus wished he could hear as well as see, but the words did not come through. Their faces grave, the men nodded to whatever the sorceress said. She crawled out through the hole. The men waited a few moments, then one placed the bomb and lit a fuse. He and his comrade ran back into the cavern toward the statues. The vision continued even after they had disappeared from it, closing in on the flame spitting along the fuse. It touched the package, and a fiery orange explosion filled Angulus's mind. Again, he couldn't hear noises, but when the smoke cleared, the tunnel had disappeared in a pile of rubble.

"Why would they have trapped themselves in here?" Angulus wondered. If they had set the rest of the explosives, they would have known that the cavern would also blow up. He couldn't imagine that the sorceress had ordered them to stay here and die. What would be the point?

His gaze drifted to Kaika. Had the sorceress guessed that Iskandians might figure out that something was going on back here and come to investigate? Possibly disarming the explosives before they went off, just as Kaika was attempting to do? If so, did that mean that the Cofah sorceress did not want Angulus's people to have access to the dragons? That killing the dragons— and her own people—was preferable to that? Then why not just blow up the cavern? Why halfway free this one and then torture it?

I do not pretend to understand the motivations of humans. You are an impetuous and illogical species.

"You're not very good at asking for help, dragon," Angulus said.

The creature let out a long breath. A sigh? Did dragons sigh? *Morishtomaric.*

"Is that a name?"

My name, yes. And I am male. Not an it.

The dragon sent another image into Angulus's mind. This

time it—he—was free of his statue prison and was flying through the cavern. Morishtomaric soared toward the rockfall, looking like he might crash, but the rubble abruptly flew outward, as if another explosion had been set off. Giant boulders arced through the air, then plummeted into a grassy valley far below. With the opening no longer obstructed, the dragon flew out of the cavern. In the vision, Kaika and Angulus ran out after him and climbed down to the valley.

Definitely a vision, since in her state, Kaika would never be able to make that climb. The slope was steep, almost vertical, and Angulus did not know if even *he* could make it down. Still, he got the gist of the offering. The dragon would help them escape, and apparently, they needed its—his help.

"Understood," Angulus said and headed toward the crystal. "Kaika, how are you doing over there?"

"Sweating. Bleeding. Making progress."

"All at once?" His instinct was not to make light of her injury, but that seemed to be what she wanted, so he went along with it.

"I like to challenge myself."

Angulus stopped in front of the glowing crystal. Though he stepped on a few broken shards as he approached, they did not crunch under his feet, breaking further the way glass would. Instead, they prodded him, slicing into the sole of his boot. After that, he took care to avoid them.

He lifted the butt of his rifle and thumped it against what remained of the glowing structure on the wall. Since it was already damaged, he expected more shards to fall away without much effort. The rifle bounced off, as if it had hit a boulder. He struck the crystal harder, but all that did was send a painful jolt up his arm.

"Uhm, dragon?"

Morishtomaric. Now that he had shared his name, he seemed adamant that it be used.

Angulus didn't know if he could pronounce it, but he tried. "Mor-ish-to-mar-ic? How did the others break this?"

An image of a silver glowing sword flashed into his mind.

"A soulblade?" Angulus guessed. "Uh, we don't have one of

those." He waved the rifle to show what he did have. Would shooting the crystal do anything?

Magic is required to break it.

"Sorry, we don't have any of that."

You wait for one who does.

Angulus scowled. The dragon had read that much of his thoughts? That was alarming, and it felt like a betrayal to Sardelle that he had inadvertently informed a dragon about her.

"I have no idea when she'll be here, and she'll be on the other side of that rockfall."

The dragon sighed again. *Remove the stakes then. Perhaps I can heal enough to free myself.* It glowered across at the crystal.

So long as it broke them free of the rock wall, as promised.

As Angulus walked back toward the box, he wondered if they truly needed the dragon's help. Once Kaika disarmed the detonator, they would have access to numerous bombs. Couldn't they use one to blow open a hole in the wall? Earlier, he had been leery of the idea of lighting charges from *within* the mountain, but one of her specialties was setting explosives for the controlled demolitions of buildings.

Safer with me, the dragon informed him.

Unfortunately, that was probably true. A bomb had already exploded at that end of the cavern, and with all of the earthquakes the dragon had caused, the walls and ceiling might have been weakened.

The dragon shared another vision, this one quick and alarming, Angulus and Kaika setting an explosive, then being buried as the ceiling collapsed.

"All right, all right," Angulus said. He didn't know if the dragon could see possible futures, but the situation seemed so likely that he believed it. "I'm going to have to climb up you to reach those lances."

The dragon hesitated, and he had the impression that Morishtomaric found the idea of a human clambering on him distasteful, but all he shared was, *Very well.*

"Who locked you up in here in the first place?" Kaika asked. She had leaned back from the detonator, which was now disassembled into about twenty pieces, with wires cut and the clock face set aside. "And when?"

"Yes, I'd like the answer to that question too." Angulus should have thought to ask it himself. That plaque on the wall might have an explanation for all of this, but it was in an old form of Iskandian that he couldn't read. His childhood language lessons had only focused on modern tongues. "Aside from a recent and unprecedented exception, it's been a thousand years since dragons have been seen in our world."

The Cofah, the dragon said. *We were protecting Oksarndiarshan, and—*

"Protecting what?" Angulus asked. He raised his eyebrows to Kaika and pointed at the disassembled detonator.

You call it Iskandia.

"Go on."

"The timer is no longer a problem," Kaika whispered in response to his gesture, "but explosives are still in precarious places and should be removed. I can do it once I—"

"No." What was she thinking? Climbing around on thirty-foot-tall statues when she had a bullet in her torso? "I'll handle it," he added.

After you pull out the stakes, the dragon said, eyeing both of them, as if to say he did not appreciate the interruption.

Angulus snorted. The dragon should be worried about deactivating the explosives too. He certainly did not appear hale enough to withstand a rockfall crashing down on his head.

"Yes, I'll take care of that first." Angulus handed his rifle to Kaika, worried it would hinder him when he climbed, then approached the dragon. Ancient instincts screamed at him that this was a foolish thing to do, that dragons had once preyed upon humans.

The wing looked to be the most promising place to climb. The way it was folded created ridges, and it draped all the way to the floor, almost like a curtain. A stone curtain. Angulus touched the bottom of it, expecting it to feel hard and cold and lifeless, but he jerked his hand back. A tingle almost like electricity flowed through the stone.

"What's that?" He looked at the box to assure himself that he had, indeed, unfastened the power cable.

Magic, the dragon said, his tone extremely dry.

Angulus rubbed his fingers and eyed the crystal. Touching the stone hadn't hurt, but it hadn't been pleasant. Maybe his ancient instincts had been justified in warning him away.

He glanced at Kaika, catching a weary and pained expression on her face. She noticed him looking and promptly smoothed her features. Her pain reminded him that she'd been shot, and even if the bombs weren't in danger of exploding in minutes, they didn't have all day. That bullet might have struck something vital.

Gritting his teeth, Angulus climbed the dragon's wing. His palms felt as if they had ants crawling all over them, but he kept going. Finding toeholds for his boots was a challenge, and it was more sheer force of will that took him to the first of the lances, rather than agility or climbing skill.

He angled toward the one thrusting through the dragon's shoulder first, both because it was closest and because it did not seem as life-threatening as the one through Morishtomaric's neck. With his feet balanced on the arm of the injured shoulder, Angulus reached for it, half afraid his footrest would move. The arm was covered in golden scales rather than stone. As he grabbed the end of the lance, the dragon remained as still as the statue he had apparently been for centuries, if not millennia. Had he truly fought against the Cofah all those years ago? Had he been imprisoned by the empire, perhaps because he had been too much of a threat? But if that was so, why would the empire have imprisoned him *here*?

Angulus hesitated, his hand on the lance. It seemed more likely that *his* people had been the ones to imprison the dragon. They were deep within Iskandian territory here. Had his ancestors done this? Then collapsed the cavern entrance so no one could find it for centuries? Millennia?

A sorcerer and several other Cofah dragons imprisoned us. We were allies to the chiefs of old, powerful warriors who defended this, our homeland, and they wanted to ensure we were out of the way for a sneak attack on your harbor. You cannot force a dragon to fly to another continent. They had to imprison us here.

"What will you do when I release you?" Angulus asked.

I wish to avenge myself upon the one who tried to torture me into helping her. An image of the golden-armored sorceress flashed into his mind.

"We could help you with that," Angulus said.

I can find her without help. Then I will slay her, and she will bother your people no more.

That was an appealing notion. Still, Angulus hesitated. The dragon could be lying to him. He looked down at Kaika, saw her gazing up at him, saw the pain in her eyes, though she tried to mask it. He made his decision.

Angulus pulled lightly on the end of the lance. It did not budge. The dragon sucked in a sharp breath. Angulus pulled harder, balancing precariously as he leaned his weight into it. The shaft slid out an inch, and fresh blood dripped from the wound. The dragon held still, but Angulus could imagine it clenching its jaw to keep from crying out. If crying out always caused an earthquake, he hoped the creature would keep on clenching.

Another inch came free, then the lance lurched as a couple of feet slid out. Angulus lost his balance and fell off the arm. Cursing, he tightened his grip on the end of the lance. His weight swung down like an anchor. The stake slid the rest of the way out, falling toward the ground, and he fell with it. He let go just before he hit and rolled away, aware of a wail escaping from the dragon and tremors coursing through the earth. He came to his feet as the lance clattered onto the rock next to him. Blood coated the steel, and droplets flew off it, spattering Angulus. They tingled where they landed on his skin, as if they were as charged with electricity as those lances had been.

"Dragon buddy," Kaika called up, "we're sorry you're in pain, but we would appreciate it if you stopped making the ground shake. If any of those bombs fall off your frozen friends' heads, they could blow up this cavern."

The quaking halted immediately.

"Dragon buddy?" Angulus mouthed at Kaika.

She'd climbed to her feet, using his rifle for support. "I'm trying to be supportive and friendly."

"So if you call me 'king buddy' in the future, I should consider that a positive sign?" Angulus approached the dragon again. Morishtomaric's eyes were still open, so he had clearly survived the withdrawal of the first lance.

"Yes." Kaika held up a hand. "I apologize for making work for you, but maybe the rest of the explosives should be removed before you try to take that other lance out. Just in case. I can guide you through taking them down." She touched her back and grimaced. Why was she even standing?

No, the dragon said. *I can control myself. I will not mewl again.*

Mewl? That wasn't exactly what Angulus would have called it. Not when the noise could shake the floor and pound his eardrums from the inside out.

"Better to be safe." Kaika closed her eyes. Her face was so pale that Angulus wanted nothing more than to carry her out of here and forget the dragon and everything else. If that rockfall weren't blocking their way, he would have done just that.

"We'll risk it." Angulus did not want to delay her medical attention. He didn't know how much time had passed but hoped Ort might be back with the others by now. If so, maybe all he had to do was get Kaika outside, and Sardelle could help her.

Nodding to himself, he climbed up the dragon again.

Control yourself, he ordered silently, though he had no idea if Morishtomaric was monitoring him.

The dragon made a noise deep in his throat, but Angulus didn't know if it was a sigh, a growl, or something else.

He made it to the top of the wing and braced himself, reaching overhead to touch the lance sticking out of Morishtomaric's throat. He had no idea where the jugular was on a dragon, but whoever had thrust the steel stake into his neck couldn't have missed by much. The placement couldn't have been accidental. The Cofah must have known what they were doing, hurting the dragon and giving him awful wounds but not killing him.

As he grasped the end of the lance, a new image popped into his mind, the sorceress standing below Morishtomaric's statue, holding one of the weapons. The other one was already embedded in the dragon's shoulder. Behind her, the crystal on the wall had been partially broken.

"It's your choice, *Morishtomaric*," she said. For the first time, Angulus heard the words spoken in the vision. "Work with us, and we'll free your comrades. Help us destroy this puny country, and we'll go back to the empire and share the rule. With our power, none will oppose us. Even the emperor himself will bow to us."

I will not work for a human, Morishtomaric responded. The lance in his shoulder did not keep him from sneering at her.

"Work for me, or I'll kill you. You'll never escape this prison. Nobody else in the *world* even remembers that you're here."

Free me or go away, human. I care not which.

The sorceress hurled the second lance, using her mind to make it strike with the power of a cannonball. The dragon cried out in pain, and the ground quaked beneath the sorceress. She stood with her legs spread, her lip curled, barely affected by the movement—or the dragon's pain.

If there had been earthquakes earlier, Angulus could see why his scientists and soldiers might have fled. They would have feared being caught in the facility with the dangerous prototypes.

"Sire?" a call came from below, cutting through the haze of the vision.

Angulus blinked a few times. He still gripped the end of the lance, but he might have been standing there without moving for seconds—or minutes.

"Yes, just receiving some information," he said. "Are you ready, dragon? I'm sure this will hurt."

You are correct.

Taking that for a yes, Angulus rose up on his toes to make sure his grip was good, then tugged. As with the other one, the lance was slow to pull free of the dense flesh and muscle. He had to lean back, throwing his weight into the effort, and he worried that he would fall again. He hadn't hurt himself last time, but that had been luck.

As the lance slipped out inch by inch and foot by foot, the

dragon moaned. The moan turned into an ear-splitting howl. Angulus tried to finish quickly, pulling with all of his might, hoping to yank it out before the dragon had time to punish the world with another earthquake. But the pain must have been too much. Even as Angulus pulled the last of the lance free, with blood spattering him in the face, Morishtomaric threw back his head and screeched. His body began to shake. No, not his body. The ground. The earth heaved, and a crack sounded deep within the stone wall behind the statues.

Cursing, Angulus dropped the lance and scrambled down to the ground. It was shaking so heavily that he could barely keep his feet. Kaika had already dropped to her knees.

Something clanked at the other end of the cavern, and he imagined one of those bombs toppling to the ground. Might that set it off? He didn't want to stay to find out. He swooped in and picked Kaika up in his arms, cradling her against his chest. She groaned, but he barely heard it over the clamor of crackling rock. A stalactite fell from the ceiling and shattered when it hit the bucking ground.

Angulus ran in the direction of the exit, the direction he had seen in the vision. It was like running on logs floating in a river. The ground heaved under him, and he kept losing his footing. Through sheer force of will, he kept himself upright with Kaika in his arms. He thought she might object to being carried, but she was so pale now. She clutched his shoulder, her eyes wide. How much blood had she lost? If he could find a way out, he could help her soon. He just hoped he could push aside the rubble he'd seen in the dragon's vision and find that tunnel before the ceiling collapsed.

Right in front of him, another stalactite broke free. It slammed to the ground, then toppled on its side like a fallen tree. It was higher than his waist, blocking the way, but somehow he found the energy to spring over it, even with the added weight in his arms. He raced around a curve in the cavern, and daylight shone in, surprising him. He spotted the tunnel opening that he'd seen at the beginning of the vision, before the Cofah operatives had lit the bomb. There wasn't a rockfall at all.

Though confused, he didn't question his luck. The quaking was subsiding, but he'd had enough of this subterranean hell. He sprinted for the tunnel.

A shadow fell across him, and he ducked, expecting another falling rock. A great draft of wind stirred his hair. The dragon shot past, his wings almost as wide as the cavern, almost scraping the sides. Morishtomaric knocked down another stalactite as he flew, then he roared, the sound deafening as it echoed from the walls. As in the vision, boulders flew outward and sailed into blue sky. The dragon shot through the opening before the rocks had settled. Even though Morishtomaric was hit numerous times, and blood dripped from his wounds, he did not seem to notice. He cleared the mountain, flapping his wings and disappearing from view.

The tunnel had disappeared, but a huge gaping hole had taken its place. Angulus picked his way around boulders, sucking in deep breaths as soon as he smelled the fresh, damp air of the forest. He wanted to rush, to sprint the last few feet, but he remembered the part of the vision that had promised this cavern came out high above a valley. Fortunately, dawn had come while they'd been inside the mountain, and he could see the way ahead. As he came out of the cave mouth and onto a boulder-strewn ledge, he spotted the dragon. Morishtomaric had already flown a mile or more and was on his way to becoming a tiny speck on the horizon, never looking back as he soared away.

The dragon had lied about the rockfall. What else had he lied about?

"Are we safe?" Kaika murmured, looking up at him, her face close to his, her arms wrapped around his shoulders.

He smiled down, worried about her, but he liked having her arms around him. "Safer than when we were inside, I believe, but we're on a ledge high above a valley."

Angulus crept forward, so he could see just how high they were.

A distant call of, "Sire!" reached his ears.

Angulus and Kaika had come out around the mountain from where they had originally entered the facility. Three fliers were sitting down in the center of the grassy valley. Even though it had to be a two-hundred-foot drop, Angulus had never been so relieved. Several people stood down there, unpacking ropes and climbing equipment. One of them had long, dark hair. Sardelle, he hoped. She could heal Kaika, and then the next time Kaika wrapped her arms around him, he could enjoy it instead of worrying she was dying.

Someone waved up at him—a gray-haired dot. General Ort?

With his hands full, all he could do was nod back. They knew he was up here, so he stepped back and found a solid piece of wall to lean against. He trusted they would find a way up to them.

"They're coming," he promised Kaika. "I think Sardelle is with them."

"You could probably set me down while we wait," Kaika said.

"Probably." But he didn't. He was enjoying the knowledge that he had defeated a Cofah operative and made it out with her in his arms. He would be feeling rather heroic if he hadn't also been tricked into letting a powerful dragon escape, one that might come back to molest his nation.

Kaika looked toward the edge where the sound of faint clinks drifted up, the men climbing up to get them. They would have to fashion a sling or some other way of bringing Kaika down. Angulus would carry her if necessary.

"Sire," she said, meeting his eyes. She bit her lip, hesitating before saying more.

He raised his brows. Was she perhaps thinking of kissing him? Or asking him to kiss her? Or maybe she wanted to profess that after giving his ass that special consideration in the tunnel, she'd decided that she wanted to sleep with him. Any or all of those things would be delightful.

"Before you're swept back up into the busy world of being a king and ruling a nation, there's something I have to ask. It's what I originally came to your castle to do, to talk *you* into doing, and I haven't accomplished that yet."

"You want to talk about your current assignment?" Angulus guessed, trying not to let his disappointment show.

"With the puppies, yes."

Was this truly what was foremost in her mind right now?

"While you're bleeding in my arms?" he asked. "I'm going to be honest. I was hoping you'd ask me for a kiss instead."

"I'm not opposed to kisses, but I need you to know that I'd go crazy and probably kill someone—one of Zirkander's pups, perhaps—if I had to stay in the city doing the same job day after day, hoping for pirates or Cofah to invade the harbor because that would be the only way I'd see some excitement."

"I know. I understand that about you now." Even if he couldn't believe she was craving more excitement after what they had just been through. She had a bullet lodged inside of her somewhere. How could that not deter a person from dreams of action and danger? "It was selfish of me to arrange that assignment for you in the first place. I'll see to it that your orders are changed, *after* you've recuperated."

The most blissful, contented smile spread across Kaika's face, and she settled more comfortably in his arms.

"You know," he said, "the city isn't a bad place to visit now and then. To recover from injuries and take in some... recreation."

"I would agree with that."

Voices drifted up, along with the sound of pebbles clattering free. The climbers were getting close.

"Sire, *this* would be the appropriate time to kiss me."

"Oh. I wasn't sure."

She wriggled her eyebrows at him.

Conscious of her injuries and that they were about to have company, Angulus lowered his lips to hers. He pressed gently, since this was hardly the time for passionate kisses that dripped with lust. Just a small taste, a brush of his tongue along her lips, a promise of more to come in the future, when they had both recovered from the night's adventures.

Kaika, however, had other thoughts in mind. Her hand slid up to the back of his head, her fingers digging into his scalp, and she turned their gentle pressing of lips into a passionate kiss that heated his blood to boiling and left his knees shaking. The wobbling knees worried him a bit, since he was supporting both of them, but he did nothing to pull back, not until they were both breathless and he had completely forgotten they were on a rock ledge waiting to be rescued.

"Do you always kiss like that when you've got a bullet in your back?" he asked, excited but stunned too.

"I promise that was just a teaser." She pulled his head closer and found his earlobe with her lips, then alternated nibbling and whispering promises of what else they would do once she recovered.

This resulted in him feeling guilty for having such lustful thoughts about someone so injured. Even so, he was completely thankful that he had shared his feelings with Kaika in the lab. He looked forward to going home very much.

That's a relief, a voice spoke in his mind.

Angulus drew back with a startled, "What?" on his lips.

Kaika paused and frowned at him.

"Uh, sorry," he said. "I thought I heard something."

When Ridge refused to give you my advice on relationships, I assumed it was a certainty that you'd never figure out how to lock lips with her.

That couldn't be the dragon speaking to him again. The dragon didn't know Zirkander. And besides, this tone was completely different, more feminine than masculine, and the words weren't thrust into his mind with so much power that they gave him a headache.

"It's nothing," Angulus said, aware of Kaika frowning at him, then at their surroundings.

She must have come to the same conclusion, because she smiled and laid her head on his shoulder.

Are you... the sword? Angulus thought to the voice in his head.

Jaxi. The tone was dry. *Mind if I poke through your recent memories to see what happened in that cavern? Sardelle and I sensed the dragon and saw it fly off, and we're trying to figure out what's going on.*

She asked you to talk to me?

Oh no. She's quite proper about not intruding in people's thoughts without permission. Since you don't even know me, she would be horrified that we're having a chat. But if you give me permission, then it would be fine, I'm sure. Besides, she'll be busy helping Kaika there. I want to know about the cavern.

I... guess. Angulus had already experienced a dragon poking around in his head. What could one more person—er, sword— matter?

You could sound more enthused. It's really quite an honor to converse with a soulblade.

Angulus didn't know what to make of the sword's humor, if this was, indeed, humor. It reminded him of the dragon's arrogance. *Is it an honor for a soulblade to converse with a king?*

I'm not sure yet. We've only just met.

At least you're honest.

I am extremely honest.

CHAPTER 9

K AIKA WOKE UP IN FAR less pain than she had been in when she had fallen asleep. Technically, she may have passed out rather than fallen asleep, because she did not remember much of the precarious climb down the cliff where she had bumped along, strapped to a big soldier's back. She didn't remember anything of what had happened after that. Now, she lay on a thin blanket, with stones and tufts of grass prodding her back. Given that her back did not hurt beyond that mild discomfort, she found the experience wonderful.

A familiar face leaned over, peering into her eyes, probably checking to see if they were still rolled back into her head.

"I'm awake," Kaika rasped, remembering the last time she had woken with Sardelle leaning over her. That had also involved being healed, back at General Zirkander's mother's house, less than a month earlier. Kaika needed to stop getting grievously injured, and she probably needed to buy Sardelle a gift. Too bad she was horrible at shopping—and even worse at gift-giving. She had a vague notion that flowers were often purchased for such occasions, but that seemed inadequate thanks for the removal of a bullet. Maybe Sardelle would like a kitten.

"Good," Sardelle said, touching her shoulder, extra healing energy flowing from her fingers. She knelt in the grass at Kaika's side, the outline of a flier just visible parked behind her. "King Angulus was most distressed when Ridge and General Ort talked him into climbing back up to the cavern instead of gnawing on his knuckles while he paced around and watched me work."

A flush of warmth spread through Kaika's body that had nothing to do with "healing energy." The words brought a rush of memories back to her, especially of Angulus confessing to her under the desk and then of sharing that kiss on the ledge.

"He's a good king," Kaika murmured, not certain if she should mention anything else. A king probably had to keep liaisons with common women secret. "Concerned about his subjects."

Sardelle's eyes crinkled at the corners. "Yes, Jaxi has been telling me about his concern."

"Jaxi? Your sword?"

"Yes. She pretends extreme disinterest when it comes to the romantic lives of human beings, yet she's usually the first to know about courting activities."

Kaika's cheeks warmed even more. How was she supposed to keep secrets from a nosy *sword*?

"He's not—I mean, we're not courting." Hells, it had only been a few hours since he'd confessed that he was interested in her.

"No? Hm."

What was that *Hm* supposed to mean? Sardelle's face didn't give away anything. Even in the middle of a castle incursion gone crazy, she wore that same serene expression, so who knew what she was thinking? The way she kept gazing down at Kaika made it seem like she expected a response.

"We might have sex," Kaika admitted. "That's all."

"Are you sure? I don't know him well, but he seems like a man who might be seeking something more substantial than bedroom acrobatics."

More substantial than sex? Like... a *relationship*? Something that continued on and on and involved people living together? Unless one counted the shared barracks at officer training school, Kaika had never successfully lived with anyone, not even her own family. It was so stifling, with the same people around all the time.

"You needn't look so alarmed," Sardelle said. "I don't think he's going to propose to you on your first date."

No. No, he wouldn't. He couldn't. Because he was the king, and she couldn't be a queen—seven gods, that was a terrifying thought. They couldn't live together, either, because he had to sleep in the castle. That was a rule for kings, wasn't it? And she would be busy on missions. He'd promised she could go on missions again.

After reasoning through this bit of logic, the feeling of panic that had arisen in her breast faded. She laid her head back, gazing thoughtfully up at the clouds in the late morning sky. Maybe a relationship where she and Angulus had their own places and their own lives could be interesting. She could go on missions, and he could do his kingly things, and then they could get together when they were both in town and boink like bunnies. She smiled, again thinking of their kiss on the ledge. It had been impressively steamy considering she had been in such pain. She also thought of the way Angulus had bested Seeker in that fight. And how, when that final earthquake had come, he had lifted her up as if she were a child's size instead of a gangly six feet, then charged out of the cavern with her amid falling rocks. That had been *very* manly. And sexy.

"You can probably figure it out as you go along," Sardelle said.

Reminded that she had company, Kaika wiped the silly smile off her face.

"Yeah." She shrugged as if it didn't matter much. "That could be fun."

An eagle soared down from the mountain, coasting across the valley toward the trees on the far side. It reminded her of the dragon and the fact that more than *courting* had been going on in that cavern.

"Has our new buddy been back?" Kaika asked.

"The dragon?" A troubled crease marred Sardelle's brow, a breaking of the serenity. "No."

"That's good, isn't it?"

"Better to know where a rogue dragon is than not."

"Rogue?" Kaika murmured to herself, testing the word in her mouth. She hadn't been privy to the entire exchange Angulus had shared with the dragon, but *rogue* seemed to fit. Mostly, she had been busy with the detonator, but she remembered the creature scraping through her mind, making her brain hurt as he seemed to read her thoughts. After that touch, she'd been oddly sympathetic toward him. She'd even told Angulus to free the dragon so he wouldn't be in pain. That wasn't like her. Oh, she might be sympathetic toward some small hurt animal, but not to a potential enemy with the power to crush her with a thought.

"We'll find out for certain soon," Sardelle said. "Jaxi is up there with Ridge and Angulus, and she'll share what she learns with me."

Kaika remembered the plaque, the language old and indecipherable. What did it contain? A warning?

The more she thought about their encounter with the dragon, the more she thought that nothing good would come from letting it go.

* * *

The cavern was a mess, with fallen rock and broken formations strewn everywhere. General Ort alternated between frowning at the dragon statues and frowning at the dead Cofah agents as he picked a route through the interior. He shook his head, made some notes on a pad, then disappeared into the small tunnel that led back into the research facility. The scientists and soldiers were supposed to be cutting their way back in through the main passage, so they could clean up and check on the projects. Zirkander had found Angulus's hand-selected researchers when he had been scouting for the secondary exit. They had, indeed, fled due to the earthquakes, deciding to wait for help to arrive before risking themselves further.

After Ort left, Angulus and Zirkander were alone in the cavern, with the general leaning against a column and looking at the big plaque next to the statues. He was also holding Sardelle's sword—that was his job, apparently, since Sardelle had stayed on the valley floor to heal Kaika's wound. Angulus had ordered the soldiers that had been brought along to stay with them. He hadn't wanted more people than necessary to know about this cavern. It might prove even more future-changing than the weapons facility, so he had only invited Zirkander and Ort to join him in here. The sword had invited herself along.

A noisy snort sounded in his head. *As if any of your people would have a clue as to how to interpret this chamber and that plaque.*

Sire, Angulus thought back.

Pardon?

It's my title. My subjects use it.

I'm not your subject. I am the mind and soul of a powerful sorceress who lived centuries before your parents ever contemplated getting randy and producing you.

Angulus rubbed his brow, wondering why he was arguing with a sword. After being awake all night, he felt crabby and punchy. He should have dropped the conversation, but he had a petty urge to get in the last word.

Sardelle is a powerful sorceress, and she calls me Sire.

Yes, but that's because she wants to be in your good graces, so you'll let her keep sleeping with her soul snozzle. I don't want to sleep with any of your subjects, so there's no need for such extreme politeness.

Her what?

Her soul snozzle. Ridge.

"Zirkander, did you know that sword has a nickname for you?" Angulus asked.

Zirkander looked startled enough to *drop* the sword. "She's talking to you?"

"Yes."

Judging by the expression on Zirkander's face, he didn't know whether to share his condolences or ask for details. "She's supposed to be looking at that plaque, not sharing embarrassing nicknames." He walked closer to the wall, drew the blade, and waved it at the plaque in big arcs.

"So you *did* know," Angulus said, tickled despite his weariness.

It wasn't clear whether Zirkander's baleful expression was for Angulus or the sword. Perhaps both.

Quit waving me around like a fly swatter, Ridge. I have news for you two.

Angulus raised his brows.

"Yes?" Zirkander returned the blade to its scabbard.

I can't read the contents of that plaque, but Sardelle can, so she's been translating.

Angulus glanced in the direction of the exit, half expecting Sardelle to be standing there.

Through me, Jaxi clarified.

"All the way down in the valley?"

Yes. Ridge, you should tell your people to read up on soulblades and links between them and their handlers, so I don't have to explain how everything works every time we bring a new sheep into the fold.

"Jaxi," Ridge said slowly, "did you just call the king a sheep?"

"It's not as bad as what she calls you. What does the sign say, Jaxi?" Addressing his question to the scabbard in Zirkander's hands was exceedingly weird.

These dragons were imprisoned here between 1403 and 702 Before Dominion. They were criminals, as judged by the humans and other dragons of the time. Murderers of their own kind and of the humans that the dragons of the period had an alliance with—the tribes who lived here before Iskandia united.

"Criminals?" Angulus mouthed, looking toward the cavern entrance, though he could not see the sky that Morishtomaric had flown off into, not from here. "Are you saying I released a murderer?"

According to the plaque, yes. That one was... Morishtomaric. One of several of this band of... there's not an equivalent in the modern tongue. Something like pirates. They killed and pillaged all across the world, enslaving humans and lesser dragons.

Angulus walked to the column Zirkander had been leaning against and used it to brace himself. He needed the support. "Any idea what the Cofah sorceress wanted with him? Or them?"

He couldn't trust the vision the dragon had shown to him. He wagered it was a half-truth at best. Still, it seemed plausible that the sorceress had, indeed, come and tried to enlist the dragons' aid. If Morishtomaric hadn't been willing to give it, she might have decided it was better to kill them all, to ensure that the Iskandians couldn't have the dragons as allies, either. She might have left her two men behind, giving them that suicide mission to ensure that none of the scientists or soldiers found their way here to do exactly as Kaika had done. It was amazing that her men would have agreed to that. Could she have some mental powers to force people to do her will? Or could she manipulate them, as Morishtomaric had manipulated Angulus?

I wasn't here, Jaxi said, *and the other dragons aren't talking.*

"Maybe we should have let the bombs go off." Angulus eyed the explosives. One had toppled to the ground, but none of them had gone off during that last earthquake. Perhaps it would have been better if they had. "Why were the dragons imprisoned if they were so evil? Why didn't the people of that time kill them?"

They're gold dragons, Jaxi said.

"So?" Angulus shrugged at Zirkander who shrugged back.

Golds were the most powerful and the natural rulers. Many humans considered them gods. You still have a dragon god in your pantheon. To kill them would have been blasphemous.

"So they've been here in this mountainside for thousands of years. Forgotten."

"Not entirely forgotten," Zirkander said. "That sorceress remembered they were here."

It's possible there were texts about the prison in her time, that it was even general knowledge to sorcerers back then, but that it's since been forgotten. I'd never heard about the place, nor had Sardelle. We didn't even sense the presence of the dragons as we were flying up. The carapaces muffle their auras. For all intents and purposes, those dragons are dead. Until the prison is deactivated, and then they're not. Jaxi offered a mental shrug. *I don't understand the magic. It's as long forgotten as the dragons.*

"So we have a criminal dragon and a Cofah sorceress roaming the country," Angulus said. "Captain Kaika's next assignment may be within our borders, rather than overseas." He would have to think about what kind of team he could send with her to even the odds. Explosives alone wouldn't be a match for either a dragon or a sorceress.

"She won't be returning to instructing my young pilots in the ways of being pulverized by grumpy ground troops?" Zirkander asked.

"She's not grumpy. She's... wrongfully placed."

"I can't imagine what that's like." Zirkander's expression twisted into one of wry regret, but he recovered soon and tapped the sword scabbard. "Jaxi's seen enough. She's given Sardelle the names of the dragons listed, so she can do some research on them if that's what you want." Zirkander stuck a hand in his pocket and regarded the remaining statues. "Do you think it might be better to go ahead and finish what the Cofah started?"

"Blow up the cavern?"

"We don't want someone else coming along to let out a bunch of criminals, do we?"

"This cavern's location is not fortuitous. With our weapons research facility so close, we don't want explosions going off next door."

"Maybe the facility should be moved. Since at least one Cofah got away, one who now knows where it is."

"I'll consider it," Angulus said.

The Dandelion facility *should* be moved, but would blowing up the cavern—and the statues within it—be the best option? If Angulus could make a deal with those dragons, such creatures could go a long way toward evening the odds against the empire. He just didn't know what leverage he could use to keep them in line or, more likely, what reward he could offer to entice them. He certainly hadn't been successful in dealing with Morishtomaric.

"I'll talk to the council," Angulus added, "and I want Sardelle's research on the dragons before condemning them to death. I also want to see what this Morishtomaric does."

"Hopefully he doesn't eat a small city."

Angulus nodded bleakly. If the dragon *did*, it would be on his head.

"Let's go, Zirkander." Angulus headed for the exit. "I want to make sure Kaika is comfortable."

"Now that you and Jaxi are friends, she'll probably give you advice on that."

"On making people comfortable?"

"On finding mutual comfort with them."

"Getting advice on *comfort* from a sword sounds appalling." Angulus was glad that Kaika did not come with a sentient sword or a magical background. Her passion for explosives seemed quite tame in comparison.

"It takes some getting used to."

"Is the advice ever apt?"

My advice is always *apt,* Jaxi butted in. *You don't exist for hundreds of years without gaining some wisdom.*

"Yes," Zirkander said, "I understand she's read hundreds of romance novels."

"Ah."

EPILOGUE

KAIKA SAT CROSS-LEGGED AT THE top of the convex
hangar roof, the harbor spread out below with the sea
and the sunset visible beyond the breakwater. The army
fort lay tucked at the base of the butte, with the city sprawling
miles to the north and east beyond it. The castle rose upon its
rocky hill at the other end of the harbor. From up here, she and
her companion had a view of the entire capital.

"A perfect place for a picnic dinner," Kaika announced,
patting the basket sitting on the roof beside her. Angulus sat on
the other side of it, eyeing the roof's slope where it steepened,
eventually dropping three stories to the runway that the fliers
used to take off from the butte. Tiger Squadron was up in the
air over the harbor now, practicing battle maneuvers, the buzz
of their engines competing with the roar of the ocean. "We can
watch the air show from up close, and this will be quite the sight
when they come in to land."

Angulus lifted a hand toward the bodyguards milling
below—one was frowning disapprovingly up at him. "The view
is stunning," he said, "but my guards seem to be concerned with
my elevation. They've been extra assiduous in their duties since
they heard that I was trapped by rockfalls and almost blown up
without them."

"So long as they don't come up here. I want to show you that
I can, indeed, enjoy a quiet, sedate dinner without finding it
boring." Kaika wanted to do more than have dinner, especially
now that there wasn't a bullet lodged in her back, nestled
perilously close to her spine. Fortunately, thanks to Sardelle,
her recovery hadn't taken long, and she would be returning to
duty soon, but not, she hoped, before she and Angulus had some
private, bodyguard-free time together.

"I'm not sure this qualifies as sedate." Angulus pointed toward the breakwater and a trail across the top of the massive black boulders protecting the harbor from the ocean. "We're higher than those seagulls."

"They're clearly chubby underachievers. Looks like someone's been feeding them bread." Kaika turned her gaze toward the sky, to the fliers and beyond. She kept expecting to look up and see that dragon sailing around. "Speaking of feeding, have there been any reports about our oldest Iskandian criminal?"

"Not yet. He may be licking his wounds. Or maybe he flew over to Cofahre to feed himself there." Angulus looked grim, like he did not expect that to happen.

Kaika gripped his arm. "If not, we'll convince him to do so."

Angulus gazed down at her arm. "At least one good thing came out of my ill-advised and inappropriately manned mission."

"You cut the throat of a Cofah operative who's vexed me numerous times?"

"That's not exactly what I was thinking of, but if I rid the world of a man who has vexed you, then I feel somewhat useful." He laid a hand on her hand.

"You were very useful. I'd crawl through a tunnel with you anytime."

A lopsided smile made its way onto his face. "That's encouraging. I'd been wondering... since the kidnapping... if I would have amounted to anything if I hadn't been born into my current position. I'm relieved that I didn't fall apart at the first sign of pressure." He patted her hand and released it. "I suppose I shouldn't be confessing such things. Women prefer confident men, I hear."

"You're confident. Just not with women. I've seen you in your element, giving speeches to the troops and negotiating with diplomats."

"You've seen me negotiate with diplomats?"

"Well, no, but I read about how you did it once in a newspaper article. You sounded very competent."

"Hm."

"Now tell me what the one good thing was," Kaika said.

His smile grew shy. "That I got to confess my feelings for you. And that you were—what was the way you put it?—checking out my ass within minutes."

"Really, Sire. I'm sure it took me closer to an hour to get around to that." Kaika patted the top of the basket. "Shall we see what kind of grub your cook packed us?"

"Very well, but I should inform you that she's a chef. She attended three different culinary academies and worked in one of the most sophisticated restaurants in the city before coming to join my staff. She might be offended to have her creations defined so carelessly."

"Are those dragon horn cookies?" Kaika had her head in the basket, and she withdrew a carefully wrapped parcel, tearing into it with childish glee to reveal chocolate-dipped treats. "They *are* cookies."

When Angulus did not comment, she looked up. He'd said something, hadn't he? About a chef. She hadn't had dragon horns in ages and had forgotten to pay attention. Fortunately, he did not appear annoyed. He was gazing at her and still smiling.

"There's something to be said for simple pleasures, isn't there?" he murmured, watching her lips.

"I told you, I'm a simple girl, Sire." Kaika handed him a cookie. Delightful smells of herbs, seafood, and bread wafted out of the basket, too, but there was nothing wrong with having dessert first.

"You can call me Angulus." He nibbled on the end of his cookie.

Kaika licked the chocolate-dipped end of her dragon horn. "What shall I call you in bed?"

Angulus coughed. Hard to believe such a little nibble of cookie could cause that reaction. "I, ah, what do you mean?"

"Like a nickname."

"I haven't noticed that Angulus shortens itself to anything flattering." His lips parted as he watched her tasting the cookie.

Kaika deliberately teased him as she enjoyed the chocolate. "No? Once we get your clothes off, I'll see what I can come up with." She surveyed him from head to toe, letting her gaze linger in certain spots.

His entire face flushed with embarrassment. She shouldn't tease him so, but once she'd gotten over being stunned by his confession and worried about what a *relationship* might entail, she'd grown quite enthused with the idea of enjoying his company in a horizontal capacity. She'd caught herself grinning more than once during her recovery, waiting like a schoolgirl smitten with her first crush for him to visit each day. Any woman would be delighted with a king's attention, she supposed, but he'd truly won her regard when he'd realized that the best place for her was out in the field, not grounded here in the capital. He understood her. What more could a girl want?

"Do you have a nickname?" Angulus asked. "Since I know you don't care for—"

She pressed a finger to his lips before he could utter her first name.

He raised his eyebrows, a hint of indignation entering his eyes. Not used to being shushed by commoners, was he? She turned the touch into a caress, tracing his lips, then trailing her fingers up his jawline to push through his hair and rub his scalp.

"I've had a handful of nicknames," Kaika said, "but since I'm picking one for you, maybe you want to pick one for me." She moved the basket out from between them and set it on her other side so she could scoot closer. "Let me give you some ideas."

This time when his brows rose, his eyes glinted with intrigue. She leaned in close, rested her hand in his lap, and gave him a kiss designed to curl his toes. Her own toes did some curling too. When the fliers came in to land, the view was probably spectacular, but they were too engaged in other matters to notice.

THE END

Made in the USA
Monee, IL
21 August 2023

41330459R00080